CW00709304

Dark Tales
Volume XIII

Edited by
Sean Jeffery

This collection first published in Great Britain in 2009 by Dark Tales, 7 Offley Street, Worcester WR3 8BH

www.darktales.co.uk

www.darktalesbooks.com

The rights of the authors and contributors have been asserted in accordance with sections 77 and 78 of the Copyright, Designs and Patents Act 1988.

ISBN 978-0-9555104-4-1

Printed by the MPG Books Group in the UK

WELCOME TO DARK TALES

Carla Grauls opens our thirteenth volume with the metallic clang of a dystopian future. Elsewhere, Priya Sharma and Desmond Meiring paint contrasting pictures of Africa, a young lad is transported to the dawn of humanity, and something far worse than cattle is lowing in the barn. And just what *is* in the freezer in the tale of a *Beast*?

Unlucky for some... But thirteen, constant reader, is lucky for you, as you are about to enjoy our finest collection yet.

Sean Jeffery - Editor

CONTENTS

CODES. CODES. CODES. CODES. I CAN'T DECIPHER THEM. I PAGE AND PAGE. WHY? WHY? MY CHEST FEELS LIKE IT IS READY FOR BURSTING. THERE IS NO LANGUAGE IN THE MANUAL FOR FEELING.

MADE FOR HIM

CARLA GRAULS

I was made for him.
Eyes: powder blue.
Lips: crimson lake.
Hair: a fine synthetic brunette.
Underneath I'm cold to the touch.
Pure metal.
The clock strikes curfew. Women on the streets of Progress City stop. The shadow of time has passed; signal received; click-click of their heels along the spotless streets. They migrate home light like feathers, perfect and unbroken.

Lips curled. Eyes set ahead. They smell like nothing. The sky is seamless and like Iris, the invention of a skilled engineer.

I look at her, pretty in her shell. I am a copy but we are coloured differently. My features are grubby, not box fresh. I stink like the filth we never see. The City is empty. My hands leave hot marks on the window. Quick step into the shop. My hem is caught on a splinter, threads run and I begin to unravel.

The fluorescent light picks up the sheen of his skin. A nametag tells me he is Fredrick.

"The curfew has struck."

"One thing, please."

He is trying to read me.

"A manual for Iris 3000."

He shakes his head, no. I blink tears, a simulation of distress. His face is unchanged. You can't fool another machine. He begins to turn away.

"Please."

"Did you *lose* the manual?"

The light bounces off his skin. His assessment is disgust but duty binds him. He takes a pen from his pocket and writes an address on a piece of paper. He folds it and hands it to me wordlessly. He puts his finger to his lips in a gesture of silence.

Smell of burning. The place of my birth. Robotic Industries. A vast workshop of simulated human. We are born into the night with the heavy sweat of hammers and stone.

Through a claustrophobia of back streets, I reach the place of Iris. I hear the clank and steel of work inside. I step to ring the bell.

A WorkerBot answers. He looks me over with an intelligence I can't comprehend. He detects a system failure.

"This is no place for you."

"I need a replacement manual."

"You don't need a manual."

"It's urgent."
I feel like my throat is crawling with insects, tighter and tighter and tighter.
He smells the filth underneath my fingernails.
"What will you trade?"
I only have one thing.
He pushes me up against the wall, his metal breath panting in my ear. He fumbles for my panties under my skirt. I feel nothing. I lost the ability of sensation 10,243 hours ago.
However filled, I'm a vessel that remains empty.
When he is finished with me, he sits silent.
"The manual?"
His face flits through a repetition of patterns. Lines appear and disappear, speaking a dialect I can't decipher.
"You don't need it."
Sharp insects crawling, crawling deeper within me.
"'We agreed to trade."
"Your human must be a master amongst his ilk."
His voice leaves a million bites along my arms, along my neck.
"What are you talking about? You don't know my master!"
My shoulders stutter.
"You're just a low-grade WorkerBot with limited functionality. Remember your place. I'm a superior model."
His face flits between two patterns.
"Yes, you are."
The WorkerBot puts the large manual for Iris 3000 in my hands. Suddenly I leak tears, unexpected, un-simulated, one in my many malfunctions.
"I never copulated with one like you."
I want to push my fist into his mouth and unhook his low-grade aluminium tongue.
Burning in my eyes.
"It was a trade."
The feeling of filth begins to spread between my thighs.

The streetlight falls yellow on me. The manual is imprinted with my black fingers. I open the pages.
Codes. Codes. Codes. Codes.
I can't decipher them. I page and page.
Why? Why? My chest feels like it is ready for bursting.
There is no language in the manual for feeling.
My functionality is dimming, dimming. I am only a small light.

I have no other choice. I ring, ring, ring the bell. It's late. I ring, ring. Please, please, please.

The only thing in the manual I could read, could understand was the address of the manual-maker.

A shadow moves behind the door. He studies the pattern beyond where I stand. It opens.

The man blinks, creases deep between his eyes. I raise my hands to him, which are in the grip of a seizure. They twist and shiver; the two traitors.

"Pl...please help. I'm deteriorating at an alarming rate."

He looks at me with sleep filled eyes.

"Come back tomorrow and make an appointment."

I grab at him, catching his sleeve with a jerk.

"Please, please, please."

He sets out his tools; long silver things with sharp ends - a family of screwdrivers and a soldering iron. Each nerve has sparked in me a violent tremor. My face and arms and legs twitch. The hem of my skirt is pulled and frayed.

He rubs his eyes and looks at me.

"How did you get those marks?"

He points to my neck.

"I don't understand. I think there's a malfunction in my nerve centre."

He takes a step closer, deep creases again in his face. His eyes widen, his mouth gapes open. Inside his mouth is a black cavern. He shakes his head over and over and over.

"No, no."

I watch him splay his fingers over his forehead, over the strands of his hair, dragging something enormous through his head.

"Who did it?"

"I don't understand."

One loose memory comes unfixed like a bloody tooth: He pokes a hole through the plastic to let me breathe. He tells me he picked me from the catalogue because he likes the way my body is shaped because I won't break easily.

His past love lies in the closet disassembled, an object in pieces after he tired of her limited capacity to bear him. Her line has been discontinued.

I learn quickly the mechanics of silence.

Except last night. After the clatter of lovemaking, I asked him. But he didn't answer. I asked him where my manual was.

MADE FOR HIM   CARLA GRAULS

The manual-maker's hands move in random jerks. This is the simulation of agitation. But it is authentic.

"I can't operate."

"Why not?"

He looks at my neck again where he sees dark shapes.

"Robots don't bruise."

Last night, I felt love for the last time when he put his hands around my neck in a familiar caress and wouldn't let go.

I was made for him.

Eyes: powder blue.

Lips: crimson lake.

Hair: brunette.

Underneath I'm cold to the touch.

Pure human.

I walk in a land barren of memory.

Copyright © Carla Grauls 2009

BEAST   C. EDMUNDS

My pink and green wellies went splot, splot, splot, as I ran across the lawn to the swing. I stopped when I got there, looked up at the sky, and opened my mouth wide to catch the rain, but none of it went in – I've no idea why not. It should've done. The rest of me was wet as wet can be, and I could feel water trickling all the way down my back.

"Found it yet, darling?" called Mummy.

Whoops. I was supposed to be hunting for the beast. I'd forgotten. I flung out my arms and spun round until I was dizzy then charged off towards the apple trees. Yes! There it was! The beast was under the bench! At first I thought it was dead, but it looked up at me and wrinkled its snout. A gurgle rose out of its throat and it sneezed.

I jumped back. How could it be alive? I didn't understand. What about all the blood, pooling around the legs of the bench and swimming away in the rain? I tried to call Mummy, but turning my head meant I was facing the inside of the hood which was silly. I pushed the hood down, even though I knew my hair would get wet, but it didn't matter – Mummy wouldn't mind – not tonight, with the rain pouring down and the thunder shaking the ground and the two of us having so much soggy fun.

"Mummy! Mummy! I've found it!"

She didn't hear me, so I ran up the path and round the greenhouse, tripping over the flowerpots as I went. Mummy was at the end of the garden, poking the rhododendrons with her pitchfork.

"Mummy! I've found it!"

She stood up and smiled.

"At last. Well done, darling. Where is it?"

"Under the bench. It's not dead though. I thought it would be dead. Why isn't it dead?"

"I must have missed the jugular. Go back into the house and get changed. You're soaked through. I'll deal with it."

As we walked back towards the bench I pulled on Mummy's hand.

"Please, can't I watch you kill it? Please?"

"No darling. Listen to it snorting and grunting. What a crosspatch! I'll be like that if you don't do as you're told. You can have a look when I've finished. Off you go."

"Okay. 'spose so."

I trudged back towards the house, kicking a flowerpot on purpose this time and jumping in all the puddles I could find to splash myself even more, which I knew would annoy Mummy, but I didn't care. I turned and scowled at the beast. It was still snuffling and coughing. Why couldn't I watch Mummy kill it? She was a spoilsport. I love watching her kill things. When I'm ten, she's said I can have a go. I'm seven and three-quarters now, so that's ages to wait.

"Lucy – get into the house!" said Mummy.

There was a flash of lightning and I could see Mummy looked very stern. Then an enormous thunderclap made the windows rattle. I shrugged my shoulders and stuffed my

BEAST   C. EDMUNDS

hands in my pockets. There was a wet hanky in one and three acorns and a pebble in the other.

"Alright, alright, I'm going."

Mummy still had the pitchfork, so I thought I'd better do as I was told. I went inside, slammed the door, grabbed a Twix bar, then ran round the back and out again.

I hid behind the cherry tree and had a good view of Mummy stabbing the beast with her pitchfork, shouting out things like: "Yes! Yes! You bastard! Take that! And that!" and lots more words that I don't know, as well as stuff about Marilyn, who lives next door – the lady Daddy used to visit. Mummy laughed as the monster squealed and tried to scuttle away, but she kept jabbing at its legs so that it couldn't get up. I forgot I wasn't supposed to be there, and shrieked and clapped my hands, dropping the Twix into a puddle by mistake.

At last, after a jab under its chin, the beast stopped squealing. I ran across to look at it.

"What a lot of blood! Mummy, can I have one of its tusks? Please? I bet Mrs Side-botham will give me a star. Emma only brings in leaves, Penny brings in conkers and nobody else ever brings in anything at all. I'm sure I'll get a star."

"Yes, of course you can, darling. Here."

She got out Stanley (that's what she calls her special knife) from her pocket and handed it to me. I knelt down in the soggy mess. I don't mind stuff like that. Games with Mummy often end up in a muddle of blood and mud and sinews. I opened the knife, facing it away from me the way Mummy's taught me so as not to cut myself, and started hacking at the monster's mouth. Hack, hack, hack, chop, chop, chop, slice, slice, slice. Mummy had to help me in the end. She said something about extractions and dentists and having sympathy.

"Don't be a dentist, will you Lucy."

"No thanks! Do dentists really have to do this?"

I shivered and carried on hacking at the beast.

"Why does it feel warm, Mummy?"

"Because it's fresh. Probably even warmer inside. Do you want to have a feel?"

"Ooh, yes please."

Mummy sliced open the belly so that I could I plunge my hands in. I could feel sausages. I got hold of them and pulled them out.

"Yikes! Look at that!" My hands were covered in slime. "Can I take this stuff to school?"

"No, darling. Have a sniff. You wouldn't want that in your 'My Little Pony' bag, would you. Just take the tusk."

"Okay then."

I put the sausages down in the mud and picked up the tusk, rolling it in my hand.

"Leave it on the bench for the rain to wash it clean," said Mummy. "Off you go, pet. I'll clear up here."

BEAST   C. EDMUNDS

I ran back into the house, leaving soggy footprints behind me, but I thought Mummy probably wouldn't mind – not after a kill. Blood and gore in the carpet happens quite often in our house. She'd probably do her dance later; the special one where she sprinkles powder on the carpet and sings to the vacuum cleaner.

I made a space for the tusk on the shelf in my bedroom where I keep all my treasures. There's a piece of flint that Mummy says was left over from making an axe; a feather from a jay; an ashtray with a picture of Tardebigge church on it, and my collection of dolls. Mummy buys one as a present for me whenever we go on holiday. I tried to make tattoos for them once with the flint. It didn't work. Jemima and Horace have swapped heads. Elspeth hasn't got a head. Boris hasn't got anything.

I took the tusk to school on Monday. I'd left it out in the rain, like Mummy said, to clean it off until the blood was gone and there was no more smell. I kept it in my pocket all morning, but wouldn't tell anybody what I was hiding until playtime. It was wet play because it was still raining. Paul was a show-off and ate a matchbox, including all the matches, but everyone preferred my tusk.

It was nature table after play. Mrs Sidebotham asked if anyone had brought anything in, and Emma put her hand up. She had a Sainsbury's bag full of wet leaves. We all

BEAST   C. EDMUNDS

laughed so much that Mrs Sidebotham had to get quite cross. She told Emma to take them outside. Then Penny showed off her latest conker. It was the biggest so far, and everyone went "Ooooh!" I didn't mind. I knew my tusk was much better. I put up my hand.

"Yes, Lucy? What have you brought? I say! Wherever did you find that?"

"It was under the bench, miss."

"Really? I wonder how it got there."

"It ran and hid."

"Now that would make a story, wouldn't it children. Jotters out! I want everyone to write a story about a tusk that ran away and hid under a bench."

"A what, Miss?" asked Joseph. He hadn't been listening.

"A tusk, Joseph."

"Like what elephants have?"

"Yes, that's right. Now, who can tell me which other animals have tusks?"

And so they went on. I ignored them. I put the tusk on my desk, and started writing my story. I could have made it up, but decided instead to tell it exactly how it happened; how Mummy and me had crept out of the house at the start of the storm when nobody else was about; how she'd freed the beast from the farm by cutting through the barbed wire, and then how we'd lured it back to our garden using a trail of food we'd left; chunks of meat and acorns and truffles wrapped up in leaves. I'd made the parcels yesterday. Mummy had defrosted all the meat that was left in the freezer and showed me how to mince it up, stir in the acorns, add some truffles, wrap it up in leaves, and then tie up with straw. You can whistle through straw. Hold a piece tightly in your hands between thumb and fingers and blow. It frightens animals and makes them run away, but sometimes they charge, so you have to be careful.

Once I'd finished making the parcels, we waited until dark, and then laid the trail. I was worried that the rain would wash the smell away, but Mummy asked me if I could smell the rain, and I said yes; and could I smell the smoke from the chimney, and I said yes; so that was alright – you really can smell things in the rain. It worked, because after Mummy cut through the wire the beast snuffled and grunted, shot past us, and started tearing at one of the parcels.

The trail led all the way back to the garden. We ran after the beast, and I ripped a hole in my sleeve on a hawthorn bush, which slowed us down. I didn't mind. It's a horrible Pacamac. Orange. I don't like orange. Now Mummy will have to buy me a new one. We lost sight of the beast in the dark, but when we got home, we knew it must have gone into the garden, because the parcel just inside the gate had been eaten. We locked the gate to trap the beast, then held hands and ran round the lawn shouting: "Piggy, piggy, we're coming to get you!" We caught sight of it and chased it into a flowerbed. Mummy slipped over on the wet grass and said a rude word. She was cross, so she went to the shed, got the pitch-fork, charged as fast as she could and managed to jab the beast.

It ran off, making a noise like a walrus being squashed by a bus, but Marilyn (that's the lady Daddy likes) wasn't at home so it didn't matter. We shouted and laughed so much that nobody would have been able to sleep, especially not Marilyn. I don't think she sleeps anyway. That's why Daddy used to visit her when everyone else was in bed.

We didn't know where the beast had gone, until I found it hiding under the bench.

I finished the story by describing Mummy killing the beast. I used lots of words called adjectives. Mrs Sidebotham likes it when I do that. Wet, splodgy, splatty, soggy, bloody, gory, trickly, dribbly, muddy, hot, sticky, smelly. I also wrote down what Mummy had shouted, although I didn't understand everything that she'd said. I forgot I was in the classroom, and just thought about how Mummy is so happy when she's killing a beast.

Then it was lunchtime, and Mrs Sidebotham collected in our jotters. Paul was sent home because of the matchbox and being sick and everything. Tristan stuck the giant protractors into Catherine's bum, and had to go and stand under the clock. It was still raining, and he said he shouldn't have to, but Mrs Sidebotham got extra cross and said it wasn't raining. I don't think she even looked outside.

Lunch was gristle. I hate gristle. I think I might ask if I can be a vegetable-Aryan next week like Jennifer Taylor. She's allowed cotted-cheese. At least we had skin for pudding.

After lunch, Mrs Sidebotham said I had to go and see Mr Reid. I don't know why. I had-n't eaten a matchbox or stuck anything in anyone. All I'd done was written a story. Per-haps it was because Paul is my friend. He gives me a Penguin at home-time on Mon-days.

"Lucy," said Mr Reid, in a voice like a blanket, "this lady wants to talk to you about your story."

The lady was a policeman. She asked me lots of questions, and filled up pages and pages in her jotter with joined up writing. When I grow up, I want to be a lady police-man, so that I can write like that. I could tell lots of stories about Mummy.

"One last question, Lucy," she said, after we'd finished going through the story for the third time: "what did you mix with the acorns and truffles in the parcels? The meat out of the freezer – do you know what it was?"

"Yes, that was the last bit of Daddy. We still had some left."

The policeman stared at me and I stared back. She turned over a page in her jotter, smiled, licked her lips, and said: "Tell me about Daddy."

A Beautiful Day in the Neighbourhood   JANICE MELARA

The sun was shining and birds were singing when Blackie, my Miniature Dachshund, and I set out for our daily walk. I glimpsed the waters of Lake Payton sparkling beyond my neighbours' homes as we strolled by. The thought of going for a nice swim after our walk briefly crossed my mind, but I quickly decided that my seventy year old body could not handle both a walk and a swim in a single day. The golden years are proving to be fun, but I do have to pace myself.

When we reached the corner of Cherokee Hill Road and Lakeside Drive I decided to go down Cherokee Hill. I usually avoid that particular street because it isn't as pleasant as the rest of the neighbourhood. It is a place where shabby older model cars and multicoloured pick up trucks splay out across unkempt yards. The rest of the neighbourhood has an air of serene comfort-luxury even-but Cherokee Hill Road feels pinched somehow. It is as if the people who live there put everything they have into just getting by while the rest of us have time for the whole gamut of pleasures that life on a lake has to offer. The road does have a long uphill stretch, though, that can't be found anywhere else. When you are walking for your health, as Blackie and I were that day, that type of feature has a certain appeal. So, we took Cherokee Hill.

Blackie stopped to pee on a mailbox post in front of one of the few houses on that street that I actually think I could live in. It is small, but neatly painted with blue shutters and an appealing roof line. When the dog was finished and we were just beginning to resume our stroll, I heard a rough male voice say, "A whole neighbourhood to pee in and he has to pick my mailbox." I looked around and saw a shadowy figure through the windshield of a blue Saturn sedan.

"Good morning," I said as pleasantly as could be.

A shirtless man, slight of build and with sandy hair tangled about his head, got out of the Saturn and answered me with a rude, "Huh."

I repeated my greeting. The man repeated his comment about my dog choosing his mailbox to pee on.

Swallowing the anger the man's tone engendered in me, I said, "I am so sorry that happened. Do you want me to clean it off for you?"

"Yeah, I do," he growled.

"Do you have some water I could use?" I asked.

"Naw, that's for you to bring," he snarled, his face screwed up into a perfect picture of hatred.

"Okay, I'll be back in a bit," I said, my voice quavering.

My blood stream had so much adrenalin floating around in it that my hands shook as I walked the few blocks home. When I got there, I considered just not going back, but I was thirsting for another encounter with the man. I wanted to give him a piece of my mind. Really, I admit Blackie shouldn't have done his business on the fellow's mailbox, but there was no reason for him to meet my apology with such rudeness. If I could only vent my feelings directly to the man, everything would be alright. Old Dr Albright, my first psychiatrist, had taught me that if nothing else.

I left Blackie at home: I didn't want him interfering when I had my little talk with the angry homeowner. As I made my way back to the trashy little house, I practised just what I would say to the ruffian. No one was in sight when I arrived, so I cleaned the mailbox off and then went up and knocked on the door. There was to be no satisfaction for me that day, though. The coward sent his daughter to the door. I knew from experience that it would do no good to tell her how I felt. It had to be the man himself or it wouldn't work.

Too bad, I thought as I toted my cleaning supplies home, *there's no telling what will happen now.* With something like this stewing inside me, I often got so worked up that I had to double up on the antipsychotic medication that various psychiatrists had prescribed for me over the years. Sometimes even that didn't work, though, and then what Dr Albright and the others called my delusions would descend on me once again.

Trying to avert a catastrophe of that sort, as soon as I got home I spread some peanut butter on a couple of Ritz crackers and poured myself a glass of milk. When I had gotten the food in my stomach, I swallowed a Mellaril and went and lay down on my bed. Usually, the Mellaril put me right to sleep. When it didn't, I knew a rough ride was ahead. Instead of drifting off to a dreamless neverland, I lay awake fantasizing about ways to get back at my Cherokee Hill neighbour. Finally, I got up from the rumpled bed. I have found that either you can sleep or you can't. If you can't, lying in bed won't change things; you might as well get up and do something useful.

The useful something that I thought to do was to look up my neighbour in our Homeowner's Association directory. His name was Rayford Lornell Pinson and his wife's name was Rue. The daughter wasn't listed, but then children never are, are they? Now that I had a name, I turned to the internet. By simply typing in a few characters, I had quite a treasure trove of information about the rude Mr Pinson on my screen in a matter of seconds. Isn't the Net a wonderful thing? In comparable situations in the past, it had taken me weeks of leg work to dig up the kinds of things I got almost instantaneously while sitting comfortably on my couch that sunny afternoon.

It seemed that Rayford—or Ray, as he was apparently called—worked for the Ford dealership in town. His surly countenance glowed up at me from under the words *Ask*

A Beautiful Day in the Neighbourhood   Janice Melara

Ray Pinson what kind of deal he can make on a new Mustang! I fought down an urge to call the Ford dealership right then and make some sort of complaint about old Ray. Planning and restraint are both essential in these matters. *After all, it could be that the Mellaril will kick in after a few more doses and I'll forget all about this whole mess,* I thought. But deep down I knew it wasn't going to kick in this time. What's worse, I really didn't want it to work. It had been a while since I'd given myself over to my 'delusion' and I missed the feeling of wildness, of downright abandonment, that I got from just letting one of my spells take hold of me.

I guess this is as good a time as any to explain about those spells. My shrinks called them 'psychotic episodes', but I looked on them as periods where I reverted to a more natural, purer form of myself.   I loved taking on that other form, that other way of being. I had always viewed it as a plus in my life, not as something to be medicated away. "Why, then, the psychiatrists and the Mellaril?" you might ask, and I would answer with one word: control. When the spells first started— when I was a young woman—they would come over me whenever I got the least bit upset about any little thing. Much as I enjoyed being able to switch between my wild self and my work-a-day self, I wanted to be the one controlling the transformation.

I tried all kinds of things to stave off spells when they cropped up at inconvenient times. Cold baths worked for a while, and a vegetarian diet seemed promising, but never really panned out. Finally, I took myself to my family doctor and described my problem. He referred me to Dr Albright, who listened politely as I explained that I wanted to be able to control my own body and mind and then nodded understandingly as he wrote the word Mellaril out on a prescription pad. "Take this every single day," he said.

I did as he suggested for a while, until I realized that I couldn't bring out what I had come to call my 'wolf-self' at all while I was taking the medication. It was when I went back to the good doctor for advice on how to let my inner self free that our differing views of my condition became clear. Dr Albright wanted to keep the beast inside me chained up for ever. I simply wanted a key to her cage.

When I discovered that I wouldn't be getting any direction from Dr Albright on how to let my wolf-self free, I began to experiment on my own. I tried cutting back my dosage of the medicine he had given me. That just gave me a sort of half and half feeling, like a sneeze that won't quite come out, or a belch that's stuck in your throat. I tried all kinds of things: warm baths, an all meat diet, an all fruit diet, green tea, black tea, and even some bitter pills I got from a Chinese grocery in the city. Finally I came upon the right formula. It was so simple I couldn't believe I hadn't thought of it right off the bat. When I wanted to unchain my wolf-self, I simply stopped taking my medicine. Then all I had to do was allow twenty four hours or so to pass and let myself loose.

Back to that trashy man over on Cherokee Hill. *I'd better get that little girl out of the house before I let myself go,* I thought. But how? How to be certain that the wife and the daughter would be gone at the right time? I had an idea, and it was one that promised to keep me occupied until I could get the Mellaril out of my bloodstream.

First, I waited a couple of days. I figured that a grouch of Mr Ray Pinson's calibre probably had interactions like the one he'd had with me at least once a day, if not more often. By the time two days had passed, he would certainly have moved on to being angry at someone else and would have completely forgotten about me. I kept taking my medicine until the following Friday, when I drove over to the city after first passing by the Pinson home to make sure old Ray's Saturn wasn't in the yard. I found a lovely little café and ate a nice lunch, then scouted around for a pay phone. It took a while, but I finally spotted one on a silver pole in the parking lot of a busy convenience store in a part of town where I wasn't scared to get out of the car.

I put my coins in the slot and listened as the phone rang once, then twice. On the third ring, a woman answered. I could only hope that it was Rue. As soon as the woman had spit out her perfunctory greeting, I began speaking, giving myself an even heavier Southern accent than I normally had. "I've got to talk to Ray," I said into the receiver. It had to be Rue. I could almost feel her stiffen up right through the phone.

"He ain't here," she answered.

She didn't offer to take a message, but I gave her one, anyway. Putting a sob into my voice, I said, "Just tell him that Billy Frank knows. He knows!"

No woman could resist that. Old Rue asked me what the Hell I meant. I was glad to explain as much as I could in the short time I'd allotted myself for the call. "Tell him he knows about us! He saw us the other day when Ray sneaked off from work!" As Rue spluttered, I moaned, "I got to go. Billy's here," and slammed the phone down.

That should be quite enough to get Ray into some hot water at home, I thought as I shuffled painfully over to my Cadillac. The arthritis in my right knee was kicking up something fierce that day.

Just to be sure my plan was working, I took Blackie for a walk that evening about dark. I gave Ray and Rue a very friendly wave when we passed by their cramped little cottage, but neither of them waved back. They looked pretty busy, what with Rue throwing things into the trunk of a battered white Honda and Ray screaming something about a wrong number as he followed her back and forth between the house and the car.

About seven that evening, I felt the change coming over me, but I held it back by thinking about anything but Ray and his rude behaviour. I watched TV. I ate a nice dinner and gave Blackie the scraps. Finally, about eleven, I knew I couldn't stave it off any longer. The change was inevitable.

I left Blackie in the house and started out walking down Lakeside Drive toward Cherokee Hill. A flashlight would have been superfluous; my night vision was already so improved that the dark country road was as easy for me to navigate as my own family room. I felt an urge to run for the sheer joy of it, but held off, knowing that action like that would only speed the change coming over me. Instead, I walked sedately over to

A BEAUTIFUL DAY IN THE NEIGHBOURHOOD   JANICE MELARA

Ray's house.

A light was on in the back of the house when I got there. I figured Ray was still up. *That's nice*, I thought. It always gives me a little extra charge to see the look on people's faces when I complete the change in front of them. I went around to the back door, knowing that is the one people out in the country tend to leave unlocked. I looked down at my hands. Although they were covered with black fur, the fingers still looked like fingers instead of claws. I used my shirt tail to cover the door knob before touching it. Sometimes I still leave fingerprints at that stage.

Sure enough, the door was unlocked. Ray was making this easy for me. Silently, I slipped into a small kitchen where six or seven crushed beer cans were strewn across the cheap Formica table. A plastic garbage pail in the corner sent out a tantalising aroma, but the still-human part of me held my inner wolf in check. It would never do to give in to such a minor temptation when the real object of my desire was just steps away.

Ray was in bed when I pushed the door to his room open. I thought I had been pretty much silent. He must have heard me, though, or maybe smelled me—I don't know which. Anyway, he looked up from the magazine he was thumbing through and screamed as soon as I set foot in the room. I was still standing upright. I looked down at my hands. They were claws now. I dropped down to all fours and started my work with Ray. The last thing I really remember clearly is how good it felt to sink my teeth into the warm flesh of his throat.

I woke up the next morning on the back porch of my own home. I was stretched out on one of the teak chaise lounges I keep out there for just such occasions. My finger-nails—when I examined them before going into the house—had a little dried blood under them, but otherwise I was completely normal looking.

After a good wash up and a hearty breakfast accompanied by a double dose of my medication, I was good as new. "Come on Blackie," I said. "Let's go for a walk!" We turned down Cherokee Hill—it did, after all, have that nice uphill stretch that is so good for one's health. There was a crowd around the Pinson home when we passed by. Two dark Chevrolet sedans with gold lettering and garish seals all over them indicating that they belonged to the county sheriff's department were parked out front.

I stopped for a minute to ask the Pinson's neighbour to the right what in the world all the commotion was about. Such a nice young man their neighbour is! "Ma'am," he said, "everybody is saying that some sort of wolf or something must have got in the house there during the night and killed Ray Pinson." I asked if he was sure it was a wolf and he said that the back door had been standing open when Mrs Pinson came in earlier that morning. She had found poor Mr Pinson in the bedroom, mutilated almost beyond recognition. There had been huge bloody paw prints leading out the door and into the woods behind the house. Just as the pleasant young man finished recounting his version of what had happened in the night, a couple of uniformed men came out of the front

A BEAUTIFUL DAY IN THE NEIGHBOURHOOD   JANICE MELARA

of Ray's door carrying between them something very heavy in a large plastic bag.

"That must be old Ray right there," someone in the crowd said. A most unladylike growl escaped from my throat. The nice young neighbour man I had been talking with looked over at me, his eyebrows raised skyward and his mouth slightly ajar. Daintily, I put my hand to my lips and said, "Excuse me! I don't seem to be feeling well at all. I think I need to get home and take my medicine."

The dear boy sweetly offered to get his truck and drive me home. "I can't imagine that it's a good idea for a frail little lady like you to be out in the sun, anyway," he said. "And it must have been a shock to hear about such a violent attack right here in the neighbourhood. It's no wonder you don't feel well." I let him drive me and Blackie around the corner in his ramshackle pick up truck. We climbed down to the safety of our own driveway. I was just about to shut the door of his ancient Chevy when the nice neighbour man leaned over from the driver's seat and warned me to be sure to keep my doors locked.

"Don't worry yourself on my account, son. I certainly plan to protect myself anyway I can," I said and then moved Blackie's little paw up and down with my hand so that it looked like the dog was waving at him as he drove off.

Discover more **Dark Tales**...

Dark Tales: Volume 12
ISBN 9780955510434
64pp £3.99

Australia and creepy crawlies feature largely in this collection, as do winged beings and, of course, Mr Grim come to do his Reaping...

I don't remember her making much noise as I clutched her calf and sunk my teeth into it—maybe a short yelp as she fell back against the wall and slid down to the floor.

...at **www.DarkTales.co.uk** and **www.DarkTalesBooks.com**

DISCONNECTION   ILAN LERMAN

Click.

She hung up on me. I guess it's over then.

The dead line is buzzing in my ear. I'm disconnected from her now. Tracy wasn't the one after all, just another manipulating witch.

"You're a scumbag, Jack. A filthy little wanker! Stay out of my life!"

I could call her right back, but the connection would still be gone. It would be like trying to mend an artery by tying it together in a knot.

Dad is sitting in his chair as usual. Beer can welded to his hand. He doesn't move an inch. He is an armchair corpse with bulging eyes. Broken blood vessels spreading like matted red hair across his cheeks. Nothing strange there, but the TV is frozen on an image of two soap opera women brawling in a pub. They are caught with mouths gaping and hair suspended in flight.

The picture flickers. To a shining round moon, then back to the frozen image.

Then I am in the kitchen with Mum. She is smoking a Regal King-Size at the table. Her face grey as ash, skin hanging in folds. I can still see the purple freckles of the bruising around her eye. They take longer and longer to heal these days.

"I'm going out, Mum," I say. "Don't lock the door, okay."

She just sits there in front of a plate of cold mashed potatoes. Ignorance is bliss. What should I expect really? She's never been interested in me. She has no idea how little I went to school in my last year. What I was doing. Who I was doing it with.

The two of you can rot in your own filth as far as I fucking care. I'll come home whenever I feel like it, that's for sure.

I blink. The picture flickers. I am walking up the road. Bungalows line the street, disappearing into the night as far as I can see. There was something weird about Mum's cigarette. The smoke was just hanging there like a cobweb. Not the permanent churning cloud above her head. No movement at all.

The night is still. Impossibly quiet. Where are the boy racers screaming hand-brake turns in Sainsbury's car park? It's Friday night.

Where are the little bastards sitting around the church steps with their bottles of White Lightning and their stupid fucking trousers hanging around their arses?

Where are the sounds of breaking glass? The midnight sirens?

If I close my eyes and listen, I can hear the sound of radio static. I can hear a deep voice in there too. A bass-heavy groaning, like the deep vibrations of music through a nightclub wall.

What? Speak up, I can't hear you.

Click.

I'm in town. Outside the Khanz kebab shop on Union Street.

Blink. Blink again. Like a strobe on its lowest frequency; the world is frozen into single frames of action.

Tony Haines and his Reebok Classic wearing twat mates are in the queue for chicken pakora. Not one of them moves. They are mannequins in a shop window displaying Friday night drunk chic.

I can move amongst them like a ghost. As fast as a leopard, teeth sharp, ready to bite.

I don't remember bringing Mum's kitchen knife with me, but it's in my hand, the handle concealed up my sleeve and the blade cold against my palm.

What the fucking hell is going on?

Guys are frozen in the middle of conversations, in mid bite of doner kebab, faces stretched in drunken laughter. I can even see the heat haze from the char-grill in the kebab shop caught in the air like Vaseline rubbed on a mirror.

Shake my head. Shake it the fuck out. Static hissing in my eardrums. Getting louder. The deep voice is speaking to me in a grinding baritone.

It's saying – *DO IT. KILL THEM. DO IT. KILL THEM.*

Over and over, thumping rhythmically in my head, a muffled dance beat pounding through me in 4/4 time.

Tune it out. Like a radio station with shite music.

Get the fuck out of my head!

Fucking Tony Haines. Kicked me so hard in the bollocks that morning in the school playground that I pissed blood. Mum had to take me to the hospital, shouting at me for wasting everybody's time.

"The doctors have got more important things to worry about than you, Jack. People have cancer, Jack. They have fucking cancer."

Tony Haines is floating in mid air. His back is arched, feet a good six inches off the ground. I can see all around and underneath him. No wires, just a solid blood sculpture erupting from his chest and I'm waving the knife around. Everyone is posed in full action, legs and arms sticking out all over the place. Mouths in mid scream, teeth bared,

spit glistening in the air like diamonds.

I can stroll slowly around them, examining their eyes, pupils dilated into punch holes, knuckles white and clenched. I can even see their words, the sound waves breaking up the air in front of their lips into spiral patterns.

Click.

I can't reconnect. *No signal, Jack.* We can't connect your call, please try again later.

I'm belting up the top of Union Street. My legs spinning in light and motion like an old zoetrope. Blood is sticking to my skin through my T-shirt. It's splashed right up to my throat.

Electric guitar feedback screeching in my ears. The strobe speeds up.

Flash. Flash.

Crashing into the top of a garden fence as I try to leap over it. My shin opens up and blood spreads out in a stain on my jeans. *My* blood this time. I feel weak, sick, dizzy.

For a brief second the night breeze rushes through my hair and I can hear the truncated blare of a police siren. Then it's gone. Weak signal, it broke through the static for a second. It was somewhere over there, over Greenlees Road or Irving Street.

Run, Jack. Lift your wooden leg and run.

Flash.

On my bed, wrapping a black T-shirt around my leg. Sweat crystallizing on my skin. A dream? No chance. There is blood caked to my clothes; the knife is jabbing into my thigh through my pocket.

How did I get here? I don't remember.

I can remember Dad smacking me over the head with the Daily Mail last week. Walloping me again and again until I had fallen on him in a rage, but I'm just a bony scarecrow, hair like thatch, arms and legs in everyone's way. He tossed me over the back of the couch like a bundle of dry sticks, dropping the paper and laying into my stomach with his fists.

"Don't *ever* fucking hit me! You skinny little no good... *Now* you've done it, you asked for this."

I faded in and out as he pounded into me, until he was just a disconnected sequence of motion like channel surfing.

That feels like ages ago now. He hasn't been able to look me in the eye since. He just hides inside a can of Stella. By the end of the night he is hiding inside eight cans of Stella and Mum won't leave the kitchen. She sits, puffs on her Regals and reads the celebrity mags; cocooned in a smoke chrysalis, dreaming of her butterfly days that never came.

I'm in front of my computer. In my boxer shorts, clean and scrubbed now. Clothes in shreds in the bin. Knife in the dishwasher. Mum and Dad are in bed.

The monitor screen pulses in and out and my head aches. The shining moon appears from a cloud of static.

It's a face. A waxing, waning, glowing moon of a face and it's telling me things. It lives in there, amongst the static, at the furthest end of the radio wavelength. Now it has found me. I'm important and it needs me.

It's saying – *JACK. KILL THEM. JACK. KILL THEM.*

My head is nodding in time to it, bouncing on a killer drum break then banging up and down. The *boom, boom, boom* of a hardcore beat. I'm lost in the music.

DISCONNECTION   ILAN LERMAN

I'm saying – *Do it. Kill them. Do it. Kill them all.*

It's in my brain, a looped sample clicking back and forth. The night plays out in front of me, images spliced together on an old film reel. The compass needle stretching my forearm skin and cutting the round shape of the moon, one on each side. Slice. Slice.

Moon Face is floating in the room, sending electrical charges into my mind to tribal dance beats.

I did it. I got away with it. I killed the smug fucker. I did it.

YES YOU DID, JACK, says Moon Face, feeding my dreams through headphones and computer graphics. In my dreams I can connect. Moon Face plugs me into everything so that I can see the action from any angle: in bullet-time, sped up, slowed down.

I am watching Tony and his mates in front of the kebab shop. They are singing football songs and then they see me and they are shouting, "Where the fuck did you come from, Jack Shit?"

I can see myself from above, moving like a cat, pouncing on him in a single swift motion, the knife flashing through the air. I am dodging around them; it's a glorious action sequence filmed in a sweeping camera motion, but then it's real.

It's real life and there's blood everywhere. People are screaming and I am running in a loping, stumbling fashion. My face is pulled into a tight circle, glowing under the streetlights, eyes wide and glassy, snot flying from my nose. I can see myself retching.

I am sweating in the dark, my bed covers wrapped around my ankles. There is too much motion, too much sound, everything is spinning, and then the tears come. I'm crying for Mum, but she won't hear. She never comes. Only in the morning when it's too late and she has to clean up my mess.

I feel six years old again, pissing the bed, screaming at shadows. Hiding from Dad.

Tune it out. Find the end of the wavelength and hide in the crackle and spit of the static. Break the connection for good.

Click. Flash.

Someone is taking pictures.

I emerge in the opening of an eye. A camera flash of bleaching light fades and I am in the busy afternoon crowds of the Lakeside shopping centre. Crouched in front of the food court, tying my shoelace. Moon Face dances in my mind, pumping out the rhythm.

Feeling good now. Moon Faces on my arms, smiling up at me.

They're saying – DO IT, JACK. IT'S OKAY. DO IT, JACK. YOU'RE OKAY.

Boom. Boom. I brought Tracy here last week. Even bought her an ice-cream.

"We never talk about interesting stuff, Jack."

She wants to talk. *All of the time.* I just want to get back to the park bench, trousers around my ankles, belt buckle clanking on the ground and do what we did that night.

"You never take me anywhere fun, Jack."

She comes to the Lakeside centre every weekend. Trying stupid clothes on with her stupid fucking friends. She wanted me to go with her, "Be a proper couple, Jack".

DISCONNECTION   ILAN LERMAN

I couldn't give a shit about make-up and hair straighteners. I'd rather be on the X-box or the PC, listening to the beat, kicking a ball against the garage door. Battering it full blast until it leaves a dent and a giant black thumb-print in the cream paintwork.

I'd like to batter it into Dad's head, leave a huge fucking dent. I'd like to take the knife and go through him like mashed potato.

The Lakeside centre is a museum of the twenty-first century. Lifelike models, all to scale, frozen in half stride: drinking coffee, pushing prams, texting their mates, withdrawing cash, shoplifting from Next.

I am a wisp of air, gliding amongst them. I can see every single one of them in close detail: the sunglasses on the lad's mag bird in front of John Lewis, her diamond Gucci watch, the fine down of blonde hair on the nape of her neck.

Flash.

Tracy is there with her mates, Ashley and Clare. Gawking in the window of a jeweller's shop at the pointless trinkets.

Boom, boom, boom. Bass in my ears. Moon Face in my head. *COME ON, JACK. NOW. DO IT, JACK. NOW.*

My vision splices. Cut straight down the middle; then again, and again. Slicing into a split screen grid where I can see every part of what happens at once.

I'm lunging at the girls, my knife colouring a pattern in the air.

Flash.

The security guards are a stone wall in my way: dark grey suits, coiled wires sticking from their ears and beads of sweat strung across their foreheads. They rise up and reach out for me.

Flash.

The knife is plunging in and out. In and out. Boom. Dance to the beat. I feel the warm sting of the security guard's blood spraying from his neck across my eyes.

Then it's all speeding up again, the stroboscope dial being turned slowly all the way to the right. I can't keep up, can't follow it.

Tracy is screaming.

I am surrounded by a wall of people that rolls away from me like a wave, leaving me kneeling alone at the centre of a crater

Then I am piling through them and they scatter like wildebeest, crashing into benches and waste bins.

I am bouncing off the tiled walls of the centre; someone pushed me in the back.

My knife whips through the air. Flash. Blood paints the window of Waterstones and a man is balled up on the floor, grasping his throat.

My mouth is wide open, as far as it can go, and all I can hear is an electronic screech that I can't switch off. The flashing and clicking and booming scaling up and up into a crescendo. Then it all explodes into white light and static.

Moon Face is melting. *I'M LOSING YOU.*

The policeman is slamming my head into the tiles. My headphones are tugged down into my T-shirt. They crunch and skitter away across the floor like a snake, trailing their black wires behind them.

Flash.

Tracy said we didn't connect. There was no spark. I can see my reflection in the mirrored panel that separates the shops; it's round and white. Like a moon.

Click.

Everything is slowing down again. Photo album snaps in a slideshow. The handcuffs are grinding into the bones of my wrists.

Flash.

I am chained to the mass of police that crowd around me, an immovable mountain range of flak jackets and plastic visors.

Time oozes over everything and sets around me. I am an insect caught in amber, handcuffed to policemen on either side of me. They are carved from rock. Light warps and bends around them. Their neck muscles stand out like rope.

I will be chained to them forever. The birds will come and peck my liver out day after day. Sorry, Mum. You'll be chained to Dad forever. I hope you can try and break the connection.

I try to blink my eyes, but this is all I will ever see now. The pause button is jammed, my screen has crashed.

Server is down, Jack. There is no signal. I can't reconnect.

A SPECIAL HAUNTING   MICHAEL LAW

It was on a May beach in Devon, a long waft of rounded pebbles stretching as far as his eight-year-old gaze could reach, that Simon first noticed the Stone.

To others it wouldn't have been worth a moment's thought. Bill, his Not-Father, would have scuffed it contemptuously aside, he knew, and got on with his quarrelling. But to Simon there was something special about it . . .

It was the end of their holiday. That morning they'd been to Kent's Cavern, near where they were staying in Torquay. He'd been clicked mechanically through the turnstile and walked obediently down the concrete paths through huge gaping caverns—black and black and hidden—where, they said, people had lived thousands of years ago, when they'd made weapons and knives and everything from stone. Now he just wanted to be home again and away from all this.

It was then that he spotted the Stone.

Walking behind his mum and Bill, his Not-Father, their giant evening shadows almost tripping him up as he went, he stopped to pick it up. And they were bickering and bickering, not noticing him, their two shadows on the beach nodding savagely, pecking at each other, shadow to crooked shadow:

"But Bill, you said – "

"No! *You* did! And what about Penelope? She deserves—"

"Penelope this, Penelope that! I'm fed up with having to consider that bloody woman— !"

Simon picked up the Stone and cradled it gently in his hands, feeling its roughnesses and smoothnesses, the barely perceptible lines still etched into it. Like feeling round a living thing, he thought. Like holding life in my hands.

At his touch the Stone seemed to move a little and shift, and he turned it round in his hands, like nursing a pet mouse, feeling with his finger-tips where the head and the body had once been.

And at the first turning . . .

At the first turning of the Stone, a great hush came down upon the world. So the thunder of waves on the pebbles was stilled to a mild murmur, soft as a honey-bee's hum. And all of a sudden the world was quite new again, though very old as well. And the bickering of the two shadows went away: Madge and Bill, Mum and Not-Father. And the sun was suddenly shuttered. Then a rushing sound. Then all at once dumb silence.

The hard stone blossoms like a flower, like a soft flower of fire in my hands as I cradle it, running. Shapes shifting . . .
    Sun a different shape, a different colour, but shining softly there still, watching over me, the Fðah of All. And the beach is now a mile long and a mile wide, stretching out and up to where I know the Cave is that I have to get to. And I'm holding the sacred Stone that shows the Holy Shape, holding it carefully in my hands as I Go Otherways.
    The beach is all great boulders now instead of pebbles and soft sand, still cradling in my hands this wild flower of stone in the shape of something I don't know; shape-shifting: part woman, part Goddess.
    Running barefoot back to the Home Cave, with Dωg leaping out to meet me, barking and licking my hand and wagging his tail, happy to beckon me back. Back to where Mðah is squatting, deftly threading her deer-bone needle to mend my hide jerkin, where I tore it yesterday on a thorn-bush. The Eldest of the Eld is there too, her face all criss-crossed with lines, but grinning. Squatting where she always squats, facing the Pot of Fire, crooning her Magic to the Fire to keep it burning softly and safely on the hearth and stop it harming others:
        "To cook but not hurt,
        Shine but not scald
        Warm but not harm . . ."
    A mile wide and a mile long. In two minds – two spaces: here and not-here. Going Otherways. . . Someone calling: 'Si! Si!' So I know I have to go along the shore; past Long Creek, where the swans nest among the tall reeds; past Great Tree on the Hill where we hang pelts of Hare and Deer, our Brωðers we love, but that we have to kill to live - and where we hang meat to dry, so we'll still have enough to eat in the Cold Times, the Lean Times when Sun hardly shows Himself and the winds blow like flint-faced knives across the land, and we huddle together, all round the Pot of Fire, to keep from freezing.
    I know what I'm carrying is very Holy. As if someone poured something into it long ago, something of the Spirit. Far back in time, far back. So it's full of this sacred thing that the people of my Tribe kneel down and worship. Always. Right up to the End of All Days.

They were still bickering and bickering over Simon's head, walking just ahead of him. Madge and Bill: Mother and Not-Father. As they picked their way crossly along that lovely Devon beach. Not noticing the rounded pebbles and the softly curling waves that washed over them again and again, a healing ritual; nor the sun going down now in a

A SPECIAL HAUNTING   MICHAEL LAW

blaze of fury, like fire, nor the great moon rising hazily like milk across the sea. Not no-
ticing Simon, until sharply:
"What's that you've got there?"
"What is it? He's always so close!"
"Put it *down*! We're not taking stones and stuff home with us, you know!"
Then back to their bickering . . .

And at the second turning of the Stone . . .
That evening, Fðah and his Hunting Mates had killed. A great Red Deer, big and big,
hiding in the bushes by Long Creek. They'd stalked it and killed it with their throwing-
spears and brought it back and skinned it and cut it up: their Brɷther they loved, that
they had to kill to live. And Bɷl the Brɷder of Fðah wears the antlers on his head and
dances in the firelight, laughing. But where is Fðah?
And Mðah cooks deer-cuts over Fire on spits of dag-wood; so our bellies are full of
good meat; and Dɷg sitting by the fire gnaws happily away on a bone. Then we sing and
laugh round Fire, blazing now with pine-boughs, throwing leaping shadows over the
Cave-walls where the tall paintings are that they say were made many many moon-
changes ago; and all the Mates drinking draughts of Mɛd and laughing, so it runs down
their beards. And one of Fðah's Hunting Mates dances, while another plays the bird-
bone whistle. And they tell stories about hunting and sing songs of love far into the
night, while above us the Stars come out to listen . . . But where is Fðah?

"What's Simon mean by 'Going Otherways', Bill?"
"How should I know? In a world of his own most of the time. A dreamer, that's what."

But Mðah shrieks: "Where is Fðah? Have we all forgotten him? Where is he?"
So they go out, all Fðah's Hunting Mates; and Bɷl among them. And when they find
Fðah lying in the tall reeds by Long Creek, they know he's given up his spirit. Then Mðah
wails and wails and tears her hair and weeps, though Bɷl tries to comfort her.
Then the Holy-man comes at Mðah's summoning, thin as a tree-pole with copper skin
and shaven head; and sits with us all in a circle round Fire. As is always done when he
comes to Truth-Tell. And he chants and speaks strange words, and scatters handfuls of
brown leaves on Fire, so smoke goes up from them through the Cave; and he leans low
over Fire, and breathes in the smoke, listening for the Voices to come to him, and his
eyes turn back in his head so all you see are the whites. And we're drowsed with the
fumes and our minds are changed, too.
Then he chants, so the Spirits can Tell Truth:
"By the Bones in the Barrow
Bones of the long-dead

Hallowed and harrowed
For weal or woe
Hearken and hear
Listen and look
Help and heal
Laid there long-past
Summoned to my side!"

And he draws pictures on slates so we see Fδah was speared by one of the Tribe, one of us. At this, a great hush goes through us and all the persons in the Cave look round, each at the others. Then the Holy-man rises up to his full height, long as a tree-pole, and with his right arm outstretched, whirls slowly round like the wheeling Sun, his Bone in his hand, pointing at each in turn: pointing and accusing and judging and Knowing. And his hand passes by me and it passes by Mδah and it passes right by the Eldest of the Eld . . . But it lights on Fδah's Brωδer, Bωl, and stops at Bωl. And Bωl is very frightened. He looks right and he looks left, to find a way out of his fright. But there is no way. So Bωl runs. Out of the Cave out of the Grove and down by Long Creek; and all Fδah's Hunting Mates after him, holding their throwing-spears and calling and whooping with the Mεd inside them; and Dωg at their heels, whiffling and baying. . .

Somehow they got him back. Although he was still Going Otherways. They thought it better. Grown-ups always did think it better, but did they know? Somehow they managed to bundle him into the car, and drive back home. Somehow.

Through the screaming traffic and the flashing lights and neon signs of the city. To the calm of the quiet suburb where they lived. And he was still Going Otherways. Babbling nonsense, they said: something about "a chase by long creek", was it? Very hot, too, when Madge felt his forehead. In between Going Otherways, he tried to tell them about the Home Cave and Fδah and his Hunting Mates. But they thought he was just making up silly stories, though he said he knew and he knew. They asked him *how* he knew. But he couldn't tell. Knowing's not something you *do*, is it? like walking or eating . . . It's a kind of feeling that comes over you.

"You've been very ill, darling!" said Madge, his mother.

"Nearly copped it!" said Bill, his Not-Father, laughing.

"But you're back with us now, you know. So you'll never need to Go Otherways ever again!' (As if she *really* knew what Going Otherways was: how silly was that!)

He wanted to ask them what they'd done with his Stone, which was two things at the same time: a lump of dead stone and a very Holy, very alive thing. But he didn't ask, because he *knew*. They'd have thrown it away before even they left that enchanted beach: "Just another of the bits of rubbish he's always hoarding!"

A SPECIAL HAUNTING   MICHAEL LAW

Then, still by his bedside: "Perhaps for Simon's sake . . ."

"You think?"

"We ought to. We ought to try, Bill."

"I'll try if you'll try."

"What do I ever *do* but try?!"

"For the lad's sake then . . . "

The voices faded as they moved away; but linked now, arm in arm, not quarrelling.

In his dreams, again and again, the Hunting Mates and Dωg catch Bωl the Brωδer of Fδah hiding deep in the tall reeds by Long Creek. And they kill him with his own flint-headed throwing-spear, driving the stone tip straight through his heart. Here. Where Simon can feel his own heart beating . . .

But when he wakes, he knows the dream isn't true: Bωl has really got away and is living here now, here under his very own roof, always here. Where he will always be, right up to the End of All Days: his own very special haunting.

Dig up more **Dark Tales...**

Dark Tales: Volume 11
ISBN 9780955510427
64pp £3.50

In this witch's brew of dark delights, prepare to read two terrifying tales with a botanical twist, a spine-chilling warning against tinkering with Mother Nature, and discover a debt with horrific consequences...

These are the type of screams you'd normally find on a delivery ward. You've noticed this isn't a birthing suite, haven't you?

www.DarkTales.co.uk
www.DarkTalesBooks.com

WOULD YOU LIKE KETCHUP WITH THAT?   S. H. HUGHES

Flint Wizbowski was a serial killer. And he liked his job.

He also made the best bagels to be found anywhere in Nosophoros City. Wizbowski's had once swarmed with customers eager for the ring-shaped bread. Now, most came for the blood.

"It's a terrible thing."

"What is, Mrs Allen?"

Flint wrapped a triangle of Gorgonzola in some foil. He knew it would keep the gooey cheese nice and moist, as it did body parts.

"The Scourge." She looked through the glass counter at the foods beyond it. "The undead running about the streets after dark has ruined my bridge nights."

"Technically, they are not undead because they've never died, Mrs Allen." He knew that contrary to the rules of zombification, those infected with the Scourge had not been reanimated after death. They were still alive. The Scourge ruined the mind first. Then the body went, piece by piece, slowly decomposed and left behind rotted corpses not given the dignity of death.

Flint watched her surveying the cheeses. The old woman was nauseating—big breasts, big hips, big mouth. He knew she would make a fine meal for those who relished such delights; she didn't match his desired profile. "Your bridge nights are legendary, aren't they, Mrs Allen?"

"Yes they are, but the players are dwindling. Mr James was attacked a few weeks ago, *before* the sun even set. Locked up his hardware store, the next minute his arm was gone. He told me he saw two of the monsters shuffling off down the street with it, munching on his fingers."

Flint knew from experience that it was not nice to watch a zombified human feed. "How is he?"

"Dead. What's that cheese there, the one in the black wax?"

"It's Dutch Gouda. The flavour is sweet and fruity, but it's an acquired taste."

"I'll try some. Yes, poor Mr James turned up at my door to play a round of bridge a week after being bitten. Of course, I could not let him in. Decomposing flesh can take your mind right off the game. So I clipped off his head with my garden shears. I keep them by the door now, just in case." She smiled and showed yellow teeth that belonged in a corpse. "I wonder where they hide during the day. What do you think, Mr Wiz-

WOULD YOU LIKE KETCHUP WITH THAT?   S. H. HUGHES

bowski?"

"Old railway stations, substructures of buildings, house cellars, if they can keep quiet enough. I mean they're not vampires, they don't sleep during the day." He glanced at her, pretended to straighten his spectacles. "I've heard." He had seen their under-world. It was a ghastly, animated graveyard of chaos.

He wrapped up the Gouda and handed it over. "Anything else?" She shook her head. "You haven't forgotten that I'm only open twelve until eight fifteen during the summer months, no weekends?" He had another job to do on those days.

"Yes, I remember. I'm sorry I've kept you tonight, gabbing on like that." She handed over her money and Flint put it in the till. "At least the sun is on our side in summer, Mr Wizbowski. Lets us walk the streets far longer than in the winter months; though it does antagonise the smell of those poor souls."

"Hurry home now. You don't want to be out after curfew, Mrs Allen."

"My home will be bolted up tight long before the sirens start." She picked up her basket of food and rushed for the door. The brass bell above it tinkled at her exit.

Flint walked slowly after her. He stopped at the door and turned the sign hung on it around to show *Closed*. His reflection in the door's dusty glass was branded by golden letters that said: *Wizbowski's Bagels and Deli*. The words *homemade pastries, cakes and cookies* had been scraped off. The deaths of his parents along with their cookery skills had lessened the counter's offerings.

He surveyed the emptying street. The sun was going down fast which prompted people to lock and bolt shop fronts quickly and dash off to their cars. He knew well that communities these days ran to the hour of sunset prescribed by the season. Those of sound mind did not wish to face the carriers of the Scourge.

Nosophoros City was now a place of bricked up entrances, locked gates and buildings gagged by security doors and window bars, some electrically charged; anything was used to keep the carriers away.

Not many dared to go out after sunset. Some did but few of them returned the same. Some never returned.

The Scourge had pushed him into daylight snatches. It was far more risky for a man of his talents. Yet he'd found that people were so careful to mind their own business, that nobody ever thought that the Wizbowskis' adopted son, now in his early forties, was doing away with members of the neighbourhood.

And why would they? He was good at his job. It was disposal that had always been a problem. To do it right you needed the freedom of the night. That had gone. In its place was curfew.

Fortunately, the Scourge had made disposal of his victims a lot easier.

The sirens wailed outside and signalled the beginning of curfew. He checked his watch, 8.32 p.m. The summer months permitted those not infected a couple of extra hours to live and work as normally as they could. Winter brought shorter working days but allowed darkness to envelope the world too soon.

Flint pulled down the door blind and switched the shop's lights on but didn't bother to turn the key in the lock. His patrons would be on their way by now. He walked back across the shop and slipped in behind the counter as the brass bell tinkled again.

The door opened and revealed the figure of Horace Grantham, or rather, what was left of him. "Flint," - his words were slurred and slow, like he'd overdosed on Prozac - "I … think … I've … found it."

Flint turned to him. "Then come and tell me all about it." He watched Horace shuffle and sway towards him like a tramp fighting against a gale. The ex-scientist's torn lab coat and filthy clothes were nothing to what the Scourge had done to his body. Flint put a chunk of Edam into the refrigerator. "What have you found, Horace?"

"A … cure," he said, words lacking any emotion.

Flint placed a slice of Brie on the shelf next to the Edam and turned to face the abomination. A sparrow flew out of a hole in Horace's skullcap and started to circle the shop. Wildlife often hitched a ride in him. "Have you been hiding in the park again?"

Horace nodded. His left eyeball popped out and dropped onto one of the tables that decorated the shop floor. It rolled over the tabletop, a sticky trail behind it on the chequered cloth. The dead eye stopped next to a bottle of olive oil. "Sorry … Flint…" Horace said, and then ate the slimy orb.

The frantic sparrow swooped over Flint and sent a breeze through what hair was left on his balding head. He came out from behind the counter, walked briskly by Horace, still trying to get to it, and headed over to the shop's entrance. He opened the door, intent on setting the terrified bird free—

Flint Wizbowski was met by a crowd of non-dead zombies.

Milky eyes stared at him, set in discoloured faces patched by dried blood, days old from the fetid stench of it. The festering wrecks came at him with open arms, as if to greet a long lost relative, tuneless moans foghorns in the silent night.

"Evening folks," he said. "Come on in and sit down, stew's almost done. No pushing. And remember, I can only seat twenty at a time."

The sparrow went by him and flew straight into the mouth of a blonde, an ex-city worker from the business suit she wore, now soaked with old blood. She snapped down her teeth and bit the bird in two.

Flint turned away from the display of bird chewing and headed back to the counter, passing Horace who still hadn't made it there yet, as the hungry crowd shuffled into the shop and sat down at the few tables available. Others crowded in until there was no space left and then the door was slammed shut.

"Now, Horace, what were you saying?"

The ex-scientist finally made it to the counter top. "Cure … found … cure …" Horace still clung to the ability to talk, unlike most of the other mindless flesh bags. The chat did take some time to get through, because he had the conversational skills of a stoned hippie, but his story remained the same. He was a dying man in search of a remedy to rejuvenate decay.

"A cure? Really?" Flint questioned.

"Try ... on ... me."

"You're going to try it on yourself? Well, it can hardly make you look any worse." Flint had often wondered if in his previous life as a human being, Horace Grantham had been a handsome man. In this current one, he wasn't even a decent corpse.

Horace was now so decomposed only a few dry flaps of flesh remained on his forehead. His teeth had held due to expensive porcelain veneers being attached to the enamel, but his lips, nose and ears were all gone. With the loss of his left eye, only a black eyehole remained in the pallid exposed skull.

"So what if this cure works?" He knew well that Horace had been working on his 'cure' for years. Scientists had created the Scourge; their want to cure the common cold had devastated humanity.

"You ... feed ..." He pointed to the packed shop of his fellow sufferers.

"You want me to feed it to the others that come in?" Horace nodded. "When will you know if it works?"

"Soon."

"Fine. Then I'll make up something special to mask its flavour, just in case." Loud moans came from the ravenous crowd. "Who's for some blood soup with fingers for dipping?" he asked them.

Fists of satisfaction punched the air.

#

Flint ran his thumb over the fingernail marks on the rusty window bar. The hunger of the Scourge had brought its carriers here. They had been right outside this bathroom window, flailing hands clawing at the security bars as they tried to get inside to retrieve the warm body within; shower steam always carried the sweetness of hot skin.

He knew the woman who lived inside apartment 3A didn't understand how much her scent intoxicated both the lost souls of the decaying non-dead and the evil ones of those who lived like him. He'd sat outside her bathroom window many times and let his olfactory senses pilfer her odour from steam as it drifted free of the pane, absorb the perfume of her cleansed flesh from rinse-water, as it gushed down the waste pipe beside him into the sewers below.

Flint held the bar tightly in his gloved hands. The blowtorch had cut through it and its three companions with ease. Now he had an entrance point. The window behind the bars was unlocked. The resident of 3A kept it that way to allow the steam to escape during her ritual of late afternoon showers.

He checked his watch - 7.55 p.m. Soon she would return to the sanctuary of her bed.

Most huddled under the blankets before the curfew sirens sang. Pills helped many off into dreams, shut down the senses and blocked the incessant noise and stench of the Scourge sufferers that roamed the streets at night.

If the occupant had popped pills to take her off into slumberland her abduction would be easy; if she had not, it would be fun. Flint Wizbowski lifted the window and climbed inside the ground floor apartment.

#

He stirred the stew. Fingers, toes and grey matter edged the whirlpool created by the wooden spoon. Flint wondered if the resident of 3A might taste better even than she had felt yesterday. The brass bell tinkled as the shop door opened. "Hello?" The sirens had not yet signalled curfew.

"Flint?"

He didn't recognise the voice. "Who is it?"

"Horace."

What was he doing out this early? "I'm in the back."

Horace pushed aside the curtain of bamboo beads that shielded the doorway between the counter and shop's kitchen, clean for a place that contained such grisly foodstuffs.

"Horace?" He had a face ... and a nose ... even lips. Tufts of brown hair patched his head and wisps of brows now arched above his eyes. The clothes were still filthy and torn, but the body beneath had muscle and skin where only bones had been on view. "You look ..."

"Human."

"Yes. But, how did you do it?"

"My cure works, Flint. It works."

The curfew sirens erupted outside. "What did you do?"

"I ate it, downed half a test tube's worth in my laboratory. Within three hours my skin had started to repair itself. After four hours I had feeling back in my body. Six hours, my features had started to regenerate and hair had begun to grow."

"What about the need for human flesh?"

"Gone."

"Completely?"

"Yes. Twelve hours after I first ingested my cure, the Scourge has been reversed. Do you understand what this means?"

It meant he no longer had an easy way to dispose of his victims.

"The Scourge will be eradicated in a matter of days." Horace took a bottle of blue liquid from his coat pocket.

"Is that the cure?"

"It's the first batch. I need more ingredients to make the next. But now I can move around in daylight, it will be easier to get." The familiar moans and shuffles of non-dead echoed out in the shop. "Is that stew for them?" Flint nodded. "Then pour this whole bottle in. It will start to work straight away. We can save these people, Flint."

"You did say you'd find a cure." He'd never believed it.

"Do you have some food here?"

"You're hungry?" Flint glanced at the pan of bloody stew. A red tipped finger floated on its surface.

"No, I mean, real food."

"There's some cheese in the refrigerator. Help yourself."

Horace went for the handle ...

Flint reached for the cleaver ...

He brought it down upon the scientist repeatedly.

The panic satisfied, Flint threw the bloodied blade into the sink, unscrewed the bottle Horace had given him and poured the liquid over it. The scientist's blue cure and blood merged, spiralled down the drain together.

Flint wiped his face clean of crimson and went back out into the shop to greet his nightly patrons.

"Anyone for a raw scientist burger with some real blood ketchup?" he asked.

A football chant of moans answered the question.

Flint Wizbowski was a serial killer. And he liked his job.

Copyright © S. H. Hughes 2009

IN THE PENGUIN COLONY M. V. WILLIAMS

On the last day of their holiday he was overtaken by an immense, unfathomable urge to see the sea again. A desire, a drive so powerful that it shocked him, swept him onwards that day as they made the journey across the hinterland towards the crowded coast.

It was a long, hot, irritating drive. The twins poked one another and squealed in the back of the car and his wife misread the map but insisted she hadn't. He didn't feel like speaking to her for the last forty miles and withdrew into glum silence. She gave him sideways looks, as if he were an unwelcome intruder in the family. Finally they arrived, parked with difficulty in the last space in the car-park and hauled their belongings out of the boot. The August sun beat down on his head. His wife fussed around the children while he picked out the heaviest items to take to the beach. In the end he carried the cool-box, the beach mats and a towel with a garishly bright sunset-and-palm-tree motif. Rolled up it still offended his eyes, but he was past caring.

"Well, you're great company," said his wife sourly.

His family straggled in an untidy line behind him as he led the way down the beach, jostling and elbowing his way towards the sea until they came to the only four-metre-square patch of sand left unoccupied. Here, a stone's throw from the sea's edge he drove their umbrella into the sand, whacking it with his shoe, then spread out their towels and beach mats and tried to protect their belongings from the gangs of marauding children and dogs and the feet of wet bathers. His wife sank heavily onto the loose sand, anchoring the beach mat. His nine-year-old son, tired and whining now to go home, sat sulkily next to her, while the twins arranged themselves neatly in a line at her side, just under the shade. He squeezed in at their feet, only partially shaded, aware that his neck was already burning from the sun. Undoing the cool-box, his wife handed each packed lunch over as though it were some prize they had won. She thrust his sandwiches out to him with a plump, rounded arm. Corned beef and beetroot, he guessed, looking at the pink juice leaking into the cling film. It smelled warm and soggy. He decided he could wait.

"I think I'll go for a swim," he said. "Save it for me?" She sighed and put it back in the cool-box with the apples, Kit-Kats, tinned drinks and packets of crisps.

"Watch how you eat that," she called to a twin, ignoring him. "If you drop it in the sand that'll be the end of it." The twin, a boy, almost dropped it, startled; then stuffed it in his mouth. His sister licked sand off her fingers.

IN THE PENGUIN COLONY   M. V. WILLIAMS

The man kicked off his sandals and picked his way carefully through the sunbathers towards the water.

The sea came to greet him with promises of cool, delightfully weightless pleasure. He submitted gratefully and launched himself through the shallows full of skinny brown children splashing and chasing one another with buckets, to where the water was a little deeper and there were youths playing ball and fooling with their dark-eyed girlfriends, who wore tiny bikinis and had water slick hair. On he went, ducking the beach balls, disentangling himself from the legs of a sedate older snorkeller, to where there was no one at all; only the blue horizon, and the hazy dark fin of an island popping up very far away. He inhaled deeply the smell of the clean briny sea. He lay on his back in the water and moved his hands a little and floated effortlessly on the undulating surface of the ocean.

This was more like it. No phone calls, no demands from his wife or his children, no one chasing up a query, sharing information or asking him to go to meetings he didn't want to attend.

He swam out a little further for the exercise, hung there in the water a while, then turned back, drifting his way slowly towards the beach, doing breast stroke, side stroke and backstroke alternately. After a while he realised he was in his depth. The youths playing ball had gone for lunch. He tiptoed along the ridged sandy bottom until he was waist deep. He looked at the beach, trying to get his bearings.

Their umbrella was red. It should be visible. He moved closer in and crouched, covering his shoulders with the water as he crept forwards. He wasn't looking forward to getting out of the sea and he put it off as long as he could. Then, stumbling up the beach he felt his full weight return to him. Dripping and self-conscious, he decided to go left, and made his way along the shoreline carefully, searching for his family under their red umbrella. He couldn't see them anywhere. He wanted to walk higher up the beach, but realised his soft feet would be burned by the sand. He had left his shoes by the red umbrella, anxious in case he should lose them on this crowded beach. After two hundred yards his back was burning and there was no sign of his family. He turned round and went back the other way, trying not to kick over the sandcastles guarded by angry little girls. There was still no sign of his family. There were many red umbrellas.

He sat at the edge of the sea as the water lapped against his toes and tickled his calves and wondered what to do. Had they left the beach without him? He decided to see if they were in the car. It was a simple explanation; they had felt ill or too burned or tired to stay on the beach. They had gone back to wait in the car. He trod with careful, scorched feet along the sand to the road, climbed over the wall and crossed over. The smell of hot melted vanilla ice cream mingled pleasantly with the ozone from the sea. Someone had dropped a cornet on the pavement. The car park he had used was along here somewhere. Gritting his teeth with pain from the loose gravel on the road, which dug into his naked feet, he looked around at the orderly rows of Fiats and Mercedes under the trees. There was his car. There was no one in it and it was locked. The sun had

IN THE PENGUIN COLONY   M. V. WILLIAMS

moved round now and it was no longer in the shade. People looked strangely at him as he stood there in his swimming shorts trying every lock on the car. It didn't look as though anyone had come back to it. The back seat was a mess of sweet wrappers and his wife's jacket was still on the back of the passenger seat.

Where could they be? They must be on the beach. Returning, he trod carefully over the hot sands with sore and smarting feet and went into the sea again to cool off. He really needed a drink. His wife had his wallet and the car keys. He had nothing.

He swam out again and floated on his back, weighing things up. He wondered if it were possible to sleep in the sea, if the water was calm enough. His weight made him buoyant and he needed little effort to stay afloat. He had heard that people from the South Sea Islands carried extra body fat to help them swim and keep out the cold. Blubber. He felt he had something in common with them. Bored by his own company, he turned his attention to his family and the red umbrella. Where were they?

Maybe the current along the shore had carried him further along this stretch of coast than he realised. He began to swim back towards the beach, a crowded horizon of seething, moving, basking bodies.

Reaching it, he clambered up the sand, which sloped here a little more than before, his feet sliding away under him, and threaded his way once more between the recliners and sun beds, the towels, mats and umbrellas, but there was nothing to say his family had ever been here. After a while he became dispirited and walked away from the sea on the hot, yielding sand, clenching his toes, towards the road, looking to see if there was a shower or a drinking water tap. Eventually he found both, though there were hornets around the drain, drinking the spilled tap water. He turned the tap on anyway, cupping his hands to get enough cool liquid into his salty mouth. There was a queue for the shower and he didn't wait.

He thought he recognised the gap in the wall where they had first come down to the beach, and, heartened, he came through it and retraced their steps over the bitter, un-reliable dust to where the bathers were. At every turn he was swerving to avoid tread-ing on someone, or dodging other bathers and knocking over someone's water bottle. There were more people than ever now, and he had to keep a tight hold on his temper. *Okay,* he wanted to shout, *I give up. Come out and show yourselves!*

He looked a little wild at this point, and his shoulders were burning badly. Sunbathers backed away as he drew close, uncertain what he might do. Even the beach peddlers didn't approach him. There was still no sign of his family, or their belongings.

He walked back and forth along the beach, from end to end. It took him most of the afternoon. He walked to the rocks where the last of the sunbathers had arranged their clothes neatly on a boulder, and back again to where the water was murky with weed on the far end of the beach. Then he swam again. He wished he had eaten the sandwich now.

People were beginning to pack up their belongings and leave the beach.

IN THE PENGUIN COLONY   M. V. WILLIAMS

In the sea again, he reasoned with himself that if he stayed in the water long enough, all the other people on the sands would go home eventually, leaving just his family behind.

He stayed in the sea for a long time, swimming up and down until a slight breeze ruffled the water and strands of dark stringy weed began to catch around his legs. He almost panicked but got a grip on himself just in time. He sat again at the water's edge and let the waves lap his calves and ankles. His feet had wrinkled, so had his fingertips, and both had the tired puckered look of white orange peel.

People walked over him, or jumped across his legs as he sat there, utterly defeated. Where in heaven's name were his family? He thought then of calling them, loudly, one by one, but felt a fool and didn't. He walked up and down from end to end of the beach again, first along the tidemark, then along the sand behind the bathers, checking every family, every umbrella.

Finally he gave up and went into the sea, floating listlessly just out of his depth. How did penguins manage it? They were all identical to look at, yet they found their way back to their colony of thousands and unerringly found the right mate, the appropriate egg; the correct territory. Without fail. How did they do it? And what happened to those that could not perform this feat? He wished he knew. At first he had been anxious about his family, then irritated, then desperate. Now he was anxious about them again, but even more concerned about his own survival.

The beach was half empty now. There was still no sign of them. An eerie thought came into his mind. What if they were a figment of his imagination? What if they had never existed? He shook his head to get rid of the idea. It was crazy. Evening crept on, as he went in and out of the sea, up and down the beach. He went back to the car several times. His belly growled with hunger and his body was sore from the sun. He had a headache that forced him to go back to the standpipe and drink vast quantities of water, like a camel. Then he sprawled on the cooling sand, face down, and slept. Above him the sky turned copper green and then indigo and the stars began their journey. Couples walked along the road, restaurant lights twinkled.

He woke, cold and anxious, and went for a last swim. The water was warmer than the night air. He felt it wrap around his tired body, comforting him. He allowed himself to weep then, for everything he thought he had and everything he had lost. The soft embrace of water felt like home.

DAIRY OF A MADMAN   TOM JOHNSTONE

December 20th

I'm listening to the boy's screams, staring out of the window at the milking shed. It seems such a desolate place since foot and mouth got the cows. But I've still got to go over there – and in this weather! John Junior's hungry. It isn't easy being a single dad!

"Alright, John," I call over to the chipped baby blue cot. "I've only got one pair of hands!" My hands are starting to twitch with rage, but I love my son.

Until her disappearing act, Brenda did all the night feeds. For me, getting up at stupid o'clock comes natural. Though the health visitor said I was a dab hand with the bottle, that busy body made it quite clear what she thought of formula.

"Breast is best," said the health visitor.

Good thing I didn't tell her what was really in the bottle!

*

I trudge through the snow to the milking shed. I feel guilty leaving him to cry in the cot, but I don't want to bring him out in this weather, and I certainly don't want him to see what's in the shed.

As I slide the metal door open, I hear it shivering from the draught, my last remaining heffer. The hole that I haven't got round to fixing in the roof has let quite a bit of water in, so the beast is huddled in a pool of icy water, but maybe this is a kindness, seeing as I haven't got round to filling the drinking trough. My hands twitch as I move towards the switch for the milking machine, which makes the creature twitch too. Then it whimpers and strains at the chain around its neck. Hardly surprising since the udder gripped in the sucker is septic with mastitis.

"Come on now, don't make a fuss," I urge. "It's time for John Junior's bottle."

"John... Please..." comes the faint reply. "I can't..."

The baby's distant screams rend the freezing night.

"Yes, you can, Brenda," I say. "Just another few ounces, then you can rest for the night."

*

I look at the bottle: barely two ounces, hardly even a few mouthfuls for a growing lad like John Junior. I go towards the door out of the milking shed.

"John," it calls feebly.

I pause.

"What is it, Brenda?" I ask patiently.

"Can I... see him? Hold him... one last time?"

"You know the answer to that, Brenda. When I found your suitcase packed, all ready for you to take my son away, you'd made *your* bed! Which reminds me, I'd better go and fetch you some fresh straw."

*

"The cattle are lowing, the baby awakes," I sing gently.
  "But little lord Jesus no crying he makes…
  "Sorry, John Junior," I soothe, "I know it's not much, but it's better than nothing. And it's like that health visitor said: 'Breast is best!'"

Copyright © Tom Johnstone 2009

CARING FOR THE LIVING   C. M. SHEVLIN

With this exclusive article, we at the Herald ask the very topical question, "Do vampires *really* make the best doctors?"

"85 year old grandmother left on hospital trolley…"
"Are you safe in their hands…?"
"Medical negligence – have you been a victim?"

Everyday headlines such as these are common. They crop up in our papers and morning TV shows, screaming a nation's dissatisfaction with growing waiting lists and the substandard healthcare they perceive as available to them. Jason Van Sangre plans to change all that. He is the public face and vice-chairman of the most recent hospital trust in the UK - Sacred Heart. The newly built hospital also has the distinction of being the first such institution to employ a healthcare staff made up wholly of the undead. We talked to Dr Van Sangre about the ethos of the new hospital, why the vampires are simply better at the caring professions and his vision for the future of the NHS.

Vampires currently make up just 2% of the UK population. Despite tight legislation which restricts their numbers to this percentage, current estimates are that at least 25% of the current healthcare workforce are undead. My first question I pose to Dr Van Sangre is why are the medical and nursing specialities just so attractive to vampires? It was a question he was evidently expecting and he smiles, showing the merest hint of fang. "It is not a hard attraction to explain. Soon after the creation of the NHS in the forties it became obvious that we'd finally found a place in human society. As you know, due to longstanding and deepseated prejudices, the undead have been ostracised and forced to live on the outskirts of human life, but here within the hospitals we can integrate and use our skills where they are most needed." That smile again. "Everybody likes to be useful."

Still sceptical, I push the point. Are vampires really suited to the so-called 'caring' professions?

"Absolutely." The answer comes quickly. "Probably more so than your average human being." His face takes on a concerned look. "Quite frankly, I worry about hospitals that don't have vampires on staff. Those with human healthcare workers daily ask the impossible of them. Young men and women who work long hours every week, asked to make important decisions with tremendous consequences at any hour of the day and night. They're expected to face harrowing situations daily, to somehow deal with dying men and women with kindness and empathy without becoming overly involved. It may seem arrogant to say but I'm very much afraid that they are simply not up to the task. Vampires, on the other hand, naturally tend to be more adaptable to the unsocial hours and have the stamina required for these demanding roles. People forget that we have been through the dying process ourselves so of course we know what it is like. We have a wealth of lifetime experience behind us and empathy with detachment is not a hard

CARING FOR THE LIVING

C. M. SHEVLIN

attitude for us to adopt." He continues, "I don't mean to denigrate the very dedicated mortal men and women who choose healthcare as their career but with heightened responses, stamina, mistakes are simply less likely to occur with vampire professionals."

Impressed despite myself, I nod and scribble a few notes while trying to think how to best phrase my next question – the one which is on everybody's minds when they think of vamp hospitals. I look up to find him watching me knowingly. "And of course, there does tend to be a lot of blood going spare." My surprise at this candour must show on my face. He shrugs. "It would be pointless for us to deny this very real advantage. Of

course we benefit from the fact that there is blood drawn for investigations that would usually be discarded, not to mention the normal losses incurred in the course of an operation or during childbirth."

"Is this why you yourself became an obstetrician?" I ask, fascinated.

"I appreciated the irony," he laughs. "Something dead helping to bring forth life. But yes, on a practical note, there is 30% more blood circulating round a woman's body during pregnancy. Most of that extra volume goes to waste during a Caesarean or a normal delivery after the baby is out. But there are ways we can harvest it and recycle so to speak for the benefit of all."

Dr Van Sangre goes on to point out that surgery is another popular speciality, and haematology of course. But he is quick to reassure that skilled specialists in every branch of medicine are employed at the hospital – from dermatologists to paediatricians.

His mood, lighthearted until now, turns serious when I suggest that patients might have misgivings about surrendering themselves to the care of people for whom they are essentially food. He leans forward over his desk and speaks earnestly, "It is extremely important that people realise we don't see them like that. It's a very symbiotic relationship. We help them and they help us. Besides if you present any 70 year old with crippling arthritis with the three available options – wait months for substandard NHS care, or pay £10,000 for a privately done hip replacement, or simply donate a few vials of blood and get top notch care immediately, I think we both know what they'd say."

I ask for a tour of the hospital and he is happy to comply. It soon becomes evident that Sacred Heart is a large self-contained complex with shops and leisure areas. There is a residential wing for staff next to the admin offices which I am not invited to tour but we make our way through the rest of the hospital. The hospital is certainly spacious although the dark-tempered windows give the building a cavernous quality despite its size. I am impressed by the pristine cleanliness of the vast corridors. Staff hurry by from place to place, in clean pressed nursing uniforms and tunics, evidently busy yet they find time for a nod and a smile. They are pale but no more so than the overworked staff of a human-run hospital. Patients are escorted in wheelchairs, the lack of natural light making them appear as pale as their carers. The hospital restaurant is loud and bustling with visitors and relatives sitting enjoying their lunch. A partition leads to the staff canteen where thermos are discreetly handed out to staff on production of their ID card. After we exit the canteen, we pass a ward round of doctors staring intently at scans on large computer screens on the wall. I comment on how normal it all looks.

Dr Van Sangre laughs and deadpans, "Well we were going to replace the white coats with swirling velvet capes to give the place a little atmosphere, but the board voted against it."

A visit to one of the wards reveals another normal scenario – beds of patients. One, Jonathan Adams, agreed to waive his confidentiality rights and speak with me.

"I have no complaints, none at all. I've had a kidney transplant. Everything has gone so smoothly."

I asked him about blood donation and his wife chips in, "He came in on the deluxe package – I donated a unit of blood and so did our two sons. It wasn't compulsory or anything, but for that, he got a few perks – private room, free cable, that sort of thing."

Standing in the large reception area before I depart, I ask Jason what his vision is for the future of UK healthcare. He admits that he is old enough to recall the NHS in its halcyon years. "A lot of us remember what it was – a service which aimed to service all the health needs of a growing population, a socialist dream. I am positive that the undead represent a life saving opportunity, if you'll excuse the pun, for the NHS for many rea-

CARING FOR THE LIVING   C. M. SHEVLIN

sons, not least of which economically. We are exempt, given our non-living status, from current European directives which place limits on how many consecutive hours staff can work. Not to mention the savings the state stands to make with regard to sick pay, pensions, etc. Imagine it—waiting lists will go down significantly, hospital acquired infections will be a thing of the past. The US has had the jump on us for a number of years – a host of vampire-run hospitals are open all over the United States, and it has been a major success story."

I remind him of the news story that broke last month in Atlanta, about St Ignatius', one such American institution, where the undead staff were accused of providing a rather radical treatment method for the terminally ill – in exchange for a rather substantial payment. His urbane smile slips. "Such a thing would be directly contrary to the hospital's mission statement. We have very strict guidelines and severe disciplinary action will be taken if any infringement of these occur."

As I leave Sacred Heart, I step out into the sunlight and blink as the harsh light hurts my eyes. Are more of these buildings the future of the NHS? I don't know but Jason Van Sangre makes a convincing argument.

THE LAST MAN IN AFRICA PRIYA SHARMA

The wind from the jet's fins flattened the tundra, cutting gullies in the sand. The captain began the descent into the long, wide valley. The jet was low enough for him to see where the baked earth had cracked, punctuated by blackened trees and dry scrub. A pack of wild dogs trailed each other in a broken brown line which scattered as the jet passed over. They were mangy mongrels that stalked close to the ground. The last time the captain had visited the farmstead the old man had offered him a piece of roasted dog meat which he took out of politeness. It made poor eating.

The jet banked, offering the captain a view of the compound. It had once been home of a fifty strong tribe but now most of the houses were gone. He could see their imprints on the land. The remains of foundations. A lone wall still standing, its door leading nowhere. The fluttering tatters of sun bleached wallpaper. An enamel bath lay half buried in sand, like the skeleton of some impossible, rotund creature. The well had been the community's heart, where villagers had gathered to talk and trade as they drew their portion in buckets, but now it was a waterless, black hole. At one time there'd been a link chain fence around the settlement's perimeter, ten feet tall and decorated in barbs. In its glory it had pulsed with electricity but now it lay inert and dirt smothered.

The jet passed over the fields, the cockpit glass slow to react to the sudden brightness reflected from below. The precious harvest was a spread of glaring light, the solar panels on fire with the morning. In the neighbouring field, where crops once flourished, were rows of solar stills. The inverted umbrellas opened at dawn, then closed with the rising sun to prevent the trapped dew from evaporating.

The captain's destination was the house and barn. He left the crew to unload the cargo and waved to the old man who watched from the dark recesses of the veranda. The captain went to him, hand out in greeting but was drawn into an embrace. The two men were like creatures of different species. The captain was pink and moist as he undid the neck of his protective suit, his smiling face a miracle of flesh and water. The old man was a different sort, a husk of wrinkled, darkened skin, his chest bare in defiance of the

THE LAST MAN IN AFRICA   PRIYA SHARMA

damaging ultraviolet. He was peppered with sinister moles, one of which he scratched.

The captain pulled his helmet right off and it hung from the neck of his suit like a severed head. Dry, hot air crackled around him. He frowned and pointed to the itchy mole
on the old man's arm. "Would you like to come back with me and get that checked?"

"No point unless somebody's going to stay and treat me."

"You could always come with me. There's a medical facility in New Atlantis."

"We'd have gills if we were meant to live underwater. I'm a land animal. I don't belong
in your new, shiny aquarium."

The old man's laughter was like water gurgling in his throat. The captain liked that.
He'd expected a desiccated sound.

"It's waterproof. I promise."

The grin again, a line of teeth in mottled browns and yellows, shaped by decay and the
old man's self dentistry. He reached up and clasped the captain's shoulder.

"Are you coming in then?"

As the captain's eyes adjusted to the dimness, the shadowy outlines settled into the
details of the old man's life. There was a cast iron stove. A table, loaded with books and
boxes. More were heaped upon the sideboard and chairs. A collection of photographs
upon a shelf, a treasured archive of the forgotten. A newborn's screwed up face and
fists. The bride's sweet smile illuminating the wedding party. A child on a rusty bicycle,
tiptoes on the floor.

The old man shifted boxes from chairs so they could sit. Despite his great age he
moved like a hunter, making the captain feel clumsy in his suit.

"I've signed all the papers."

"I know. I just wanted to say goodbye."

The papers stated that the old man understood the consequences of staying but before he'd been allowed to sign there had been psychiatrists to certify his sanity. He had
put the base commander to a great inconvenience.

"I'll not change my mind, so don't waste your time on my account."

"I know." The captain nodded as the old man waved a cup at him, offering hospitality.
"We're the last plane. There's no-one else left."

"Except for me. You military types don't like loose ends, do you?"

The captain flushed, stung by the remark. The old man noted his discomfort with a
chuckle. He turned the tap of the barrel and water trickled into the cup with a splutter
that became a gush.

The subdued lamps flickered into darkness before jolting back to life. The captain esti-
mated the output from the solar field. Plenty for one man. He could feel the floor
boards trembling, the storage cells beneath abuzz.

"Your wiring's faulty. Are you sure we can't sort that out for you?"

"No. I don't want your boys crawling all over the place, messing things up. Besides, it'll give me something to do."

They sipped their water. It was rude to gulp it down in company. Something hung from the arm of the old man's chair, something the captain had never seen before. He reached out and unhooked it. It was a wide strap of animal skin, toughened by age. The lustre of the pelt had gone. The old man had cut a hole in one end and threaded twine through it to make a hanging loop.

"Like it?"

"What is it?" The captain couldn't decide on its origin. Not dog or rabbit. It was more hair than fur.

"It's a scalp."

The captain turned it over, feigning nonchalance. He was a soldier after all.

"They'd come looking for oil and water. And women. Sometimes they'd snatch one. If we were lucky they'd eventually abandon her and we'd find her wandering out there, beyond the fence. There are things I'd kill to protect. Things I killed to avenge."

The captain put the scalp down on the table, wanting, but not asking to wash his hands.

"What happened?"

"A band from the north. Lucky for us that they only had spears and bows, not guns. Most ran on foot but their leader had a horse, a beauty the colour of ripe corn." He sighed. "I never asked his name. His hair was long, in matted braids and he wore a necklace of bleached bone."

"It sounds like you admired him."

"That's respect. Respect and fear your adversary if you want to stay alive."

The captain nodded at this piece of wisdom.

"There were nine of them. They breached the fence. The sentry was strangled as he dozed. We kept dogs back then. They more than earned their keep that night. It was them that sounded the alarm. In the end, the bandits couldn't match us. We shot four of them outright. They hadn't expected us to have rifles. But damn that man and his horse. We chased them off but he doubled back. Rode up my porch steps and right into my house."

The image of the half naked rider filled the room. His jewellery, made of finger bones, rattled with the stamping of the horse's hooves. The old man's wife, neither of them so old back then, cowering against a wall. He twists her wrist and the knife drops from her hand.

"By the time I got back, my wife was slung before him on the saddle. As I took aim, the horse leapt from the top step and I had to roll away or he'd have trampled me."

"Did she run away?"

"No." The old man arched an eyebrow. "I brought her home."

"Alone?"

"It was the village rules. Taken was gone for good, unless it found its own way back."

"My God."

"You think we were harsh. The well, the livestock and the crops had to be protected at all costs. Without them, no-one would survive."

"What did you do?"

"I wasn't allowed to take a gun in case it fell into their hands. So I took my longbow and a knife. Five men, a woman and a horse weren't hard to track. I caught up with them by the next nightfall. A lot can happen to a woman in a day. Swaggering and arrogant, they lit a fire." He winked. "No respect or fear. It was a beacon. It helped me find them in the dark."

The old man got up for more water. The captain refused a second share.

"I garrotted the watchman, like for like. The wire bit into his neck like it was butter or soft cheese. He tried to shout but all that came out was a whistle of air. I used his blood, still hot, to paint my face.

I shot the second in the eye. It pierced his brain. He hung his head in death. The third pitched into the fire, my arrow embedded in his chest. When he started to scream on his funeral pyre I had to use haste. I raced into the firelight and to dispatch the fourth with my knife. He was slower than the rest. My blade slid into his underbelly and spilled the content of his bowels into the dirt."

"Was that the leader?"

"No. He was running back from where he'd been lying with my wife." The old man took the piece of his enemy and hung it back on the chair. "I keep this to remind me. I shouldn't be allowed to forget. I didn't just kill him. I hurt him first. I severed the tendons of his arms and legs him captive. Then I peeled off most of his skin. Stuffed thorns under his fingernails and into his eyelids. Then I poured dry sand into his nose. I bled him slowly to keep him weak, but not so much as to kill him. Do you know how long you can keep a man alive?"

The captain shook his head, looking at his fingers that lay laced upon his lap.

"Five days. It would have been longer but I sickened of myself. She begged me to stop. She could no longer watch. We loved each but it broke something between us."

"I never heard that story."

"We never told anyone."

He's confessing, the captain thought, *while there's still someone here to absolve him.* His own wife and daughters came to his mind. The safe confines of the base and the order that awaited them in New Atlantis. Lives that didn't necessitate such a personal sort of violence.

He wanted to tell the old man that he didn't admire him any less for this revelation. These once-suburbians had found themselves pioneers in a hostile land. Of those who stayed, fewer still survived, marooned in a newly made wilderness, subject to nomadic raiders and the cults of the sun gods and the gun.

Instead, the captain said, "A man does what he must."

"Yes, but he doesn't have to be proud of it."

They sat in silence for a while. There was nothing more to be said.

"What are they doing out there?"

The old man had gone to the window and raised the blind. The crew were outside, their white suits dazzling in the violent sun. They were moving supplies from the jet's belly to the barn. These were plain boxes, not the meagre military relief crates that had already been delivered, signed and countersigned for.

The captain handed the inventory to the old man who took it without comment. Written in the captain's sprawling hand, it was a list of what he'd managed to collect by bribery, trading, scavenging and favours owed. There wasn't much to spare but he was proud of what he'd been able to procure. It made him feel better. He owed it to the old man. There was a rifle and bullets, drums of oil, matches, aspirin, antibiotics, bandages, a cable of wiring, needles, thread, clothes, a blanket, cases of salted fish and meat.

"You can still change your mind, Granddad." The captain hadn't intended to ask again. "You could leave with us now."

"You're just like your father. He was always going somewhere. He hated it here," the old man sniffed, "and he was always ashamed of me."

The captain didn't contradict him. He wouldn't belittle him with pretence.

"He thought about you, right at the end."

The old man pointed to the cemetery plot beyond the barn where the dead had been buried in the old fashioned way. The line of headstones cast oblique shadows. Their surfaces had been scoured by the wind and sand until the crudely cut names were softened and blurred.

"I had six children and they're all buried here except for him. I don't blame him for wanting to go. Or not wanting to come back." He shook his head. "A man shouldn't outlive his children."

The captain's father had been cremated, his ashes scattered, free to roam. That was how the captain remembered him: always leaving.

"Here." The captain held out a photo. "My wife and children."

He ducked his head, shy as his grandfather took it, his chin disappearing into the neck of his suit.

"Can I keep this?"

"Yes, it's for you."

"This one's like your grandmother." The old man pointed at the youngest child and then at a picture on the wall. The continuity of genes was remarkable. "See that bed, back there?"

The bedroom door was ajar, revealing a sliver of bed, neatly wrapped in a sheet. "I was born there. I carried your grandmother there on our wedding night. Your father was born there and that's where she died."

A sun storm was coming. The crew responded to the frantic signals from their suits and took refuge in the jet as it blew over. Solar rays broke in blinding flashes on the ground.

The old man pulled the blinds down and turned up the lamps. The captain could make out more detail on his sagging chest, a totem of tattoos from navel to neck, the extinct recalled in inks on skin.

"You can go. You've done your duty by me. I'll not leave."

"Come with me. You have a family."

"You owe me nothing." The old man picked up the scalp again. "I'm not your grandfather. He was."

The captain sat down, stunned.

"We were sure, before you ask. I tried to make your dad mine but I don't blame him. He was always troubled. It was in his blood."

"It doesn't matter now. You have a place with us. Don't you understand? Nobody's left. You're all alone. You'll die alone."

"Look around you. I *am* alone." He touched the captain's arm, as if it pained him to tell a young man such an ugly thing. "Ultimately, we all die alone."

The captain wanted to argue although he knew it was true. He had been with his father when he'd died. In his last moments his breath became erratic, fingers fluttering over the quilt, but his eyes were far away, going where his son couldn't follow. His father was a nomad, even in death.

"You can't possibly know," the old man said, kindness in his voice.

"What?"

"What it was like here once." He leaned forward as though they were conspirators. "It was paradise."

Outside there was only dry earth and scrub for miles and miles.

"I remember when there was a television in the village." Television and motorcars, mountains of paper and plastic, all come to nothing. "We gathered round to see the broadcast of the last man in Africa."

"I don't know much about that." The dead continent had long since passed into myth.

"Why would you?" The old man was talking aloud but his mind's eye drifted. "They filmed him, the last man to leave. He must have been a great warrior or a king. This African was magnificent. Head and shoulders above every other man there. His skin gleamed.

"He looked like he was leaving a person, not a place. He got on his knees and kissed the earth and when he stood up he was clutching a fistful of dirt. He stood before the plane and said, 'I'm part of this land and it's part of me. I've seen lions stalk the antelope and elephants pause to caress the dry bones of their dead. They're gone and now I will be gone. There's no-one left to remember.'"

The news reel had run its course. The old man was back in the present, the captain back in focus.

"Do you understand? I've had a lifetime of saying goodbye. To my wife. To my children. Even to my worst enemy. If I go, who will keep them company? This used to be the garden of England. Cattle grazed in the meadows. Rivers glided under the cool shade of trees. There were foxes, roses and bumblebees. Rain like you've never seen. Not floods but rain that poured itself into the ground to nourish it. And good hearted English drizzle that kissed your face. I played in that as a boy. Have you ever seen rain like that?"

"No." Of course the captain hadn't.

"And even though nothing remains, I'll stay here to remember. I'm too old and sentimental to say goodbye."

The old man waved them off, scorning the sunlight. The captain watched from the cockpit, searching for regret or panic, but none came. He just waved and waved as the jet became a silver streak fast enough to pierce the very blue of the sky itself.

Copyright © Priya Sharma 2009

See what else has been conjured up at **Dark Tales**...

Dark Tales: Volume 10
ISBN 9780955510410
52pp £3.50

In this edition, **Dark Tales** veteran Niall McMahon returns with his wonderful *Rainy Day*, Merlin the magician puts in a refreshingly original appearance, and the arts world serves as the backdrop for two chilling tales. Read also about murderers, ghosts and sci-fi star **David Brin**.

She kisses me full on the lips. I can taste her death. She does not know that on another plane she has been consumed.

www.DarkTales.co.uk
www.DarkTalesBooks.com

THE DEADLY SEMICIRCLE   DESMOND MEIRING

The lion mocked Reid. But then the Kenya bush often outsmarted you, played a trump card. Reid had tried to get Johnson a good male lion for a week, from their camp by the Gurumetti River. Barry Johnson was a cold fish, a multi-millionaire so powerful that he seemed to transcend any specific nationality. A trophies man, he got what he wanted. His wife Carolyn was elegant as a fashion-plate, even in her comic wide-brimmed hat with its anti-gnat veil. She was a trophy too.

That dawn was the second in which Reid had led his two clients stooped through a game tunnel to his bait. One zebra lay and the other hung from an acacia tree to hold the lion when he was semi-gorged. But they saw only two hyena. Scavengers moved fast in Africa. Vultures and Marabou Stork ringed the bait too, squat and dead-still on the branches like obscene fruit. Sated, they would lollop away ungainly as drunks, too full to take off. Others gathered gracefully above them, swinging in the high steel blue on jagged-edged black wings, pinpointing these deaths.

"So no lion, again!" said Johnson scathingly.

"Still, I got some great shots of the hyena!" volunteered Carolyn, so happily that they all laughed. She was a video-camera fiend.

But Reid understood Johnson's obsession with lion. He always tried to get his client a good lion early in the safari. It did wonders for the morale, not that Johnson ever lacked that. In fact the lion was usually less dangerous than the leopard, buffalo, rhino and elephant. But his *mana* was tremendous. He was as highly charged across history as the bull, and more widely spread. The lion was the 5000-year-old motif of the Cylinder of Suze, the sculpted companion of the Princesses of Nineveh, the immense stone guardian of the Royal Terrace at Angkor Wat. The Assyrians had trained him to hunt for them 1000 years before Christ. Henri Rousseau painted him in florid savagery. He was the true pagan king, able to take full grown ox in his jaws over a seven-foot fence. What less, indeed, would satisfy Barry Johnson?

So late that afternoon when the heat of the sun had eased, Reid took his party down to the river, near the bait. They saw the lioness at once. Reid stopped the Land Rover. The lioness lay statuesque, facing them, her gold cat's eyes fathomless. Too young cubs gambolled by her. She glanced at them and they lay down. Carolyn in the back seat peered out ecstatically to film. The lioness must have seen that. She got up, her cubs echoing her. She stood regally, sleek muscles still, fine grave head motionless, ears pricked at this intrusion. Her tail's tip flicked slightly, but with all the impact of a raised ministerial eyebrow.

"Should I shoot her?" asked Barry Johnson.

Reid swung round, appalled. "No! No. You'd hardly want that skin."

Shutting Johnson out, Reid looked back at the lioness. Such sudden sights justified his life. He had always hunted for the freedom and Kenya's beauty, not for the heads. He had his rewards. For no one knows the land so well, in its dawns and nights, breathtaking grandeurs and murderous furies, in all its textures as can the hunter. So with huge secret laughter Reid saw the lioness nudge her cubs. They trotted off obediently into the thick bush. She followed, long smooth muscles rippling, taking her time; no one was pushing her out.

"Maybe off to warn her mate," said Reid. "We'll try new ground."

He stopped at a ridge above a swamp, covered by tall Kikuyu grass.

"Mboga!" said Kolokolo in Reid's ear, pointing with his chin. He was Nandi, cousin to the Masai, tall slim, with fine Nilotic features, ear-lobes pierced. He could lope forty miles a day, Reid's best gunbearer ever.

"Meaning?" asked Johnson. It was his safari and he wanted full value for his money.

"Buffalo," replied Reid. "Down there, see?"

"They're *dreamy!*" exclaimed Carolyn. "Those lovely droopy horns!"

"Worth shooting?" queried Johnson curtly.

"Either bull, yes. You've two on your licence. Keep your mind off lion, anyway. So let's go!"

The seven buffalo eyed them warily from 100 yards into the grass. It buoyed up their heavy black-barrelled bodies like grey water. Reid and Johnson each took a finely-balanced Holland and Holland .470 double-barrelled rifle and four fat heavy cartridges from the car. "They'd stop a tank!" observed Johnson. "A charging buffalo's just as dangerous," replied Reid. "And don't just ignore me!" added Carolyn. "A camera can be lethal too!"

As they moved from the car the buffalo broke, and planed like black speedboats through the thick grass. One bull stayed in a small clearing, steady as a statue, front legs apart, head lowered, needle-pointed horns menacing, great bosses shielding his skull; no shot here. Often they lost sight of him. He could take off at any time too. Sixty yards from him, Kolokolo hissed and pointed left: a black-maned lion padding off. Reid cut savagely at the .470 at Johnson's shoulder—"Far too far off! Stick to your target!" Johnson's handsome face contorted. He looked like murder; Reid's.

Meanwhile the buffalo was round and away. Reid heard the vicious twin roar of the .470 next to him, saw the buffalo falter, then barrel on into the thick bush ahead. He spun round enraged on Johnson.

"That's really handy! Two late gut shots! Now we have to go into dense bush to finish him! Or he kills the next damned fool who comes along! Next *wait* till I tell you to shoot, will you?"

"Hell, a guy can make a mistake, can't he?" exclaimed Johnson. "Who's paying for this safari, anyway?"

"If you don't like the way I'm leading it," Reid said icily, "we'll strike camp for Nairobi tonight. I'll get you a refund."

"Derek!" cried Carolyn. "Take it easy, *please!*"

She and Reid had been on first-name terms from the start. Not so Reid and Johnson. Carolyn went on at once with her peace mission—

"I got fine shots of Barry firing, anyway. You too. And the buffalo."

She got her laugh again.

"Great!" said Reid. "But please wait at the car this time, Carolyn. There's no light for your camera where we're going!"

Indeed, it seemed subterranean, the thick matted bush where the buffalo had dissolved. Nearly blinded, you stopped every few yards to look, listen, feel. You filtered every shifting puff of air, sound or vibration, reorienting yourself by sudden intuitive twists into immobility. Reid put Kolokolo ahead, far the shrewdest in this game-tunnel's world. Kolokolo tracked by the patches of bloody froth waist-high. That meant wounded lungs. A buffalo so wounded could go miles. Theirs could be anywhere here, turning his horns' points onto them. A wounded buffalo usually did a lethal semicircle on his pursuer. Reid knew that theirs had done just that when Kolokolo found no more blood. So he turned their small group back.

Reid respected the African buffalo. Left in peace, he might indeed look dreamy to Carolyn, but he was really mean when hurt. Reid had once spent hours up a thorn tree avoiding one. Reid had gone alone into deep bush when a client, like Barry, had gut-shot a bull buffalo who'd then done his favourite trick, a silent deadly semicircle, till he breathed down Reid's neck. Reid had dropped his rifle and leapt for a branch. He spent the hot day dodging the buffalo who stood on his hind legs like a performing elephant. Had he reached Reid's feet his sandpaper tongue would have licked them to the bone. The buffalo had very decently fallen over dead just before Reid's gunbearers found him.

Now Barry Johnson's wounded buffalo burst out of the tunnel's right like a black whirlwind. Incredibly, Barry fired his two shots instantly, reloading in a flash—unnecessarily. Nor did Reid shoot. The buffalo, a bulky muscled statue in black marble, simply stood, then made a sudden terrific lunge forward, as if in a last heroic attempt to get at his killers. At last he lay with his head on his forelegs, like a dog on watch. The tips of his horns touched Barry's toes. His eyes glazed. He'd fought his best fight.

"You don't need any second trophy," said Reid. "These horns tip to tip are about forty-eight inches, near record. We'll have your name up in the Norfolk Hotel yet!"

"Near record!" repeated Barry. He loved that. He looked at Reid penetratingly. "You didn't shoot at all yourself?"

"No," replied Reid. "He's all yours."

Back at the hunting car, Reid extolled Barry's final shooting. Carolyn was somewhat flippant. "You always were a lucky devil, Barry!" she said. "But really you owe it all to this strong lifeguard here!"

She smiled bewitchingly, her hand on Reid's forearm. The triple battery of that smile and her two breasts in décolleté impacted him, with her provocative perfume. Barred from their hunting-party, she was rigging up her own one instead. Reid guessed Barry bored her to death, if not his money. Barry, lips tight, eyebrows solid, eyed Reid bleakly. *Don't blame me!* thought Reid, nettled. *Look, all's fair in love and war!*

Chat was light on the way home. Reid bumped the Land Rover across the veld between conical anthills. His headlamps pinned impala, kongoni, Tommy and Grant's Gazelle, wildebeest, zebra, kudu, even eland. Most stood mesmerised, eyes yellow or a witch-like orange-red. Impala broke away in exquisite parabolic leaps, a joy to see.

Supper was a good deal more sociable. Bathed, and in clean pressed clothes, they sat in comfortable camp chairs drinking whisky by a roaring great wood fire. They were man's history in miniature, clinging to their tiny lucid clearing against the surrounding predatory dark jungle. That pre-dawn, indeed, Reid had shown the Johnsons the pugmarks of a big male lion between their tents and his, and up to their flaps. Reid glanced at Barry Johnson. Threats could come from within the clearing too.

"And what was the lion you wouldn't let me shoot?" asked Johnson.

The lad didn't forget his grievances, noticed Reid. Two Africans, in smartly-ironed bush-shirts and shorts, set down the dinner of rich Tommy meat and veg. "*Felix massaica,*" replied Reid, "a Highlands lion. Too big for the semi-desert *leo somaliensis*. Anyway too far to shoot."

"I really can't see why we *haven't* got a lion yet," said Johnson, still nit-picking. "Since we've got all the rest. Even buffalo!"

"Don't underestimate it," said Reid. "Sin of pride. We were lucky."

"Of course you've not always been a white hunter," said Johnson.

Reid smiled at the implied disparagement. "Still, I was born and grew up here. So I've hunted more than most. You'll get your lion!"

"I hope you've read the small print," said Carolyn, "or he'll sue you for millions! Have your head on a plate!"

One afternoon when Johnson slept she had talked to Reid about him. She suspected even his manic fitness, his excellent squash and golf as really just social assets. She preferred Reid's tenacity, bred from many exhausting chases across this splendid bush. And Johnson usually killed in committee, liquidating a man's career and often his deepest self-confidence with a golden handshake, not by a more honest bullet.

"And it's a good head," she went on, "I like it's laughter-wrinkles!"

Barry Johnson's face showed no such frivolities. It was bland.

"Even like this?" asked Reid, trying to keep the party blithe. Hatless, he was cherubic. By day his bush-hat left his face below it deeply sunburnt, his skull from the ears up very white.

"The top part looks like a monk's cap," said Carolyn.

Reid laughed. "Don't count on that too far!"

"No, indeed!" interjected Johnson aggressively. "I'd say Mr Derek here has mighty strong male urges. From his looks at you, say!"

In the ugly silence, Reid went pink up to his papal cap. "Just a tribute to a lady's great beauty," he said. But Johnson had more to say: "And *cunning!* Don't forget that! Really pitiless *cunning!*"

"You just can't stand anyone approaching your property, can you?" asked Carolyn bitterly. "Or what you *think* is your property!"

Johnson examined her closely. "Well, if that's how you want it. So, no more champagne and caviar, of course. Better get used to that!"

It was the coolest declaration of war Reid had ever heard. He refilled their whiskies and called Kolokolo to set things for 5 a.m. The firelight bounced off Kolokolo's bare shins. The bait was still there.

"And will there be a lion?" asked Johnson. Kolokolo's high Nilotic features brooded down on him. "Yes!" Reid translated both ways.

"Great!" said Carolyn. "I'll record the whole drama on my video!"

The lion must have heard her. His roar broke, five miles or five yards away. It froze their sinews with fear. The night was the lion's.

But others moved in it too. Reid received Carolyn at 2 a.m. She was volcanic, and at least as fit as her husband. Her waist was flat and her breasts pointed upwards. Her nipples were as assertive as a political party's rosettes. They made love for an hour. Only after it did it strike Reid that neither had said a word of endearment. Some passions were too imperative to admit any frills.

Johnson, clean-shaven and bush-jacketed, seemed impeccable at pre-dawn coffee. But he avoided Carolyn's eye. Reid sensed his cold fury. He took them in cautiously, dropping a handful of dust. It fell vertically. The lion couldn't scent them. They took the two .470s. Anti-gnat hatted, Carolyn trailed with her camera. *Wait*, dear lion!

He did. He lay Trafalgar Square fashion by the lower zebra, gorged, nine-foot-six and 400 pounds, pure tawny save for his bloody mask. Those voracious undertakers, vultures and Marabou Stork, ringed his tree. Reid saw no mate; odd. He sign-called to Johnson to shoot. The lion saw that, for he stood at once, heavy muscles of his shoulders rippling, jaws opened in that paralysing guttural roar. He bunched low to charge. Reid half-saw Johnson behind him shoot and re-load immediately, just to his right. The two big expanding bullets struck. The lion collapsed, deep gutturals gone, claws tearing again and again into the ground. The splendid cat's eyes still pierced them, all in seconds.

Carolyn screamed horribly. Reid spun round. The lioness was on top of Johnson, holding him, her hind claws like a leopard's disembowelling him. Reid shot her as she ripped out Johnson's throat. His carotid arteries spewed, subdued when they knelt by him. As was Johnson. Reid heard just one outraged bleat: "Beaten by a goddamned *female*!"

Reid wondered which he meant. He saw Kolokolo, alert, unsurprised.

Carolyn shook when she stood. Reid walked her out. "The lioness stalked us from the side," he said, "another deadly semicircle!"

"Yes, as I was filming. She flew across like a crack in the lens."

"Look, I'm very sorry about Barry's death."

"Don't be. He was aiming at the base of your skull when I screamed."

"God Almighty! But of course, it adds up! He hated competition, like last night's. Well, you wanted out, didn't you? You've got it!"

"Sure. And with all his fortune now, not nothing. I'm *free!*"

"So he'd have passed off my murder as just another hunting accident. But how'd you then get any money from him?"

She patted her video. "I'd have filmed him killing you, remember?"

"My God, brilliant blackmail! You've buttoned it all up nicely!"

Of course she wouldn't *have screamed warning when Johnson first took aim to kill me,* thought Reid, *but only when the lioness had already hit him.* For Reid had swung round exactly when the lioness was already de-gutting Johnson. In the split seconds before she had condoned Reid's murder. Yet who could prove it? Her scream hadn't been recorded. And filming was not a capital offence. It made Carolyn a thorough lady working in from the blind side lethally, even elegantly. Reid would prefer a wounded buffalo in deep bush any time. It could always fall dead. Not Carolyn.

"What were we saying just now?" Reid asked her. "About deadly semicircles?"

© Desmond Meiring 2009

NIGHT SEA JOURNEY TO TURKU   GEORGE BERGUÑO

To the memory of William Heinesen

The taxi that swept onto the Stockholm pier on that warm damp evening in August was a shabby old thing. It rattled along and pulled up alongside the Narvik – a ship bound for Turku. From the interior of the cab a youth emerged, bearing pale lips and anxious blue eyes. Shouldering a small bag with clean shirts, shaving implements, a packet of cigarettes and a book of Homer's verses, he boarded the ship. A moment later, the gangplank was removed, the foghorn gave its eerie blast and the ship left the pier.

The youth, who was a native of Copenhagen, had been wandering up the eastern coast of Sweden for three days – first by ferry, then by bus – for no other reason than to go as far north as possible before the summer ended. But upon arriving at Stockholm, he had decided that he would visit Finland. He told himself that he had always longed to see Helsinki and so the change of plan was entirely justified. The fact was that he had never given a thought to that mysterious country of lakes and forests; but he was a youth like any other, filled with the magic of self-deception.

Knowing that the crossing to Turku was an overnight trip, he approached the ship's steward – a broad-shouldered man with a neatly trimmed dark moustache – and requested a cabin for the night. The man with the dark moustache studied the youth carefully before replying, as if the request itself were an unusual event on this ship.

"You should have reserved a cabin," the steward barked. "This is the busy season. Most passengers will be sleeping in the lounge and restaurant tonight."

The youth made his way down the labyrinthine corridors of the ship, climbing from deck to deck, but the steward's prediction had come true: the ship was surging with tourists, and it seemed the youth would never find a secluded corner in which to lay his head down for the night.

In the lounge, a jazz band was playing and couples moved to the shrill, plaintive tones of a saxophone. Repelled by the frantic contortions of the dancers, the youth made his way to the restaurant in search of a quiet table where he might sip some wine and let his thoughts meander. But no sooner had he entered the dining area, than an unhappy incident took place. A fat man fisting a mug of beer collided with the youth, the beer spilling onto the youth's jacket. It was if the restaurant itself were rejecting him, demanding that he be gone. The fat man apologized for his clumsiness. Holding the beer mug with one hand, he brushed down the youth's jacket with the other. But to the young man it seemed as if the coarse bloated hand that was trying to make things better was pummelling his chest.

He fled from the fat man; he ran away from the crowds, threading his way from room to room and staircase to staircase, until at length he reached the deserted upper deck, where he resigned himself to sleeping under the gentle shimmering of the arctic stars. Sprawling his tired body onto a deckchair, he rummaged in his bag and found his cigarettes. He smoked lazily, and gazed out at the murky green waters of the Baltic Sea. In the distance: the faint lights of Stockholm – and the long arms of the setting sun glided on the waters, like a red and orange flower that refuses to wither.

All at once, he knew he was not alone.

A woman stood with her back to the sea, her fingers gripping the handrail. She was a tall woman of about forty, with weary eyes that seemed to peer out from deep in their sockets; only her long dark-brown hair stirred to the gentle caresses of the night breeze. She wore a long grey dress that reached down to her bare feet. A golden chain with a solitary pearl adorned her slim pale neck.

"May I have a cigarette?" she asked.

The youth sat up. Reaching into his bag, he brought forth the packet of cigarettes and offered it to her. But she remained standing, her eyes riveted upon his face. Seeing that she made no effort to take the proffered cigarette, he withdrew his arm and remained sitting with the packet in his hand, silent and confused.

"Where are you going?" she asked.

He hesitated before answering, "Helsinki." Then, after a longer pause, "I've always dreamed of going there."

"I've always been making my way to Helsinki," she said. "But I've never been able to complete my journey."

Then, as the youth pondered the woman's strange words, an extraordinary thing occurred. It was a moment of pure magic that he would remember time and again over the years, and recall on the day he died. The woman turned her head and looked down the length of the deck, revealing her magnificent profile. And as she did so, the sun gave one final desperate burst of light before it sank into the waters. The rays of the dying sun shone on the woman's hair, giving it a red tinge that transformed her. She became another woman, full of the splendours of youth; a woman of about eighteen years, eyes blazing with life, limbs poised for a dance.

The woman with the red-brown hair skipped gracefully to the deckchair next to the youth. She sat so close to him, he could smell her fragrance, see the brown of her eyes and hear her rapid, shallow breaths. His throat parched, his hands trembled, his heart pounded.

"Aren't you afraid to be up here all alone, without anyone in the world to guide you?" she asked.

He looked down at his shaking hands, not daring to meet her gaze.

"I like to be alone," he said at last.

"I'm always alone."

They dug into silence like soldiers in their trenches. The Swedish flag crackled in the wind. The black velvet night shone brighter than the glaring white stars.

Suddenly, the woman rose and said, as if speaking to the wind, "The hour is late. Where are you staying tonight?"

"I have nowhere to go," he said mournfully. "The cabins are all taken and I can't stand to be with the other passengers."

"You'll catch cold if you stay here. You'd better come with me."

The woman's cabin was a cramped little box, with a narrow bunk and no electricity. Only the light from the stars at the other end of the universe, as it climbed through the porthole, allowed them to see their way in the dark. They lay naked, their bodies like parallel tracks, tense and burning for each other. She lay inert, encased in her mystery – like a jewel well set. At length the silent lovers were lulled to sleep by the gentle rocking of the waves and the distant clatter of the ship's engines. His sleep that night was deep; it reached into the very bowels of the earth.

When he woke next morning he found he was alone; the ship no longer rolled from side to side. He heard the shuffling of hurried feet and knew at once that the Narvik had set anchor. He dressed hastily, slung his bag over his shoulder and set about looking for his companion of the night. But the mad scramble to disembark had already begun and it seemed to the youth that every woman that he glanced at was the woman with the blazing red hair. He stared at the passengers, watched as they clawed their way down the gangplank, yelling and shoving, until only he remained. Was she still on board? Surely, she would not have left without exchanging farewells!

He descended into Turku, looked for her in the narrow lanes of the ancient port, sat in restaurants and coffeehouses, waiting. He wandered through the grounds of Turku Castle until the day grew bleak and tired. At dusk, he boarded the train to Helsinki, arriving a minute before midnight. For three days he searched for her in the dreary grey-stone avenues of the capital city. He waited by the harbour, took his meals standing in the Old Market Hall, prayed in the cathedral on Senate Square. By and by, he grew desperate and boarded the train to Joensuu. He searched for her by the lakes, roamed the forests by day, the lonely city streets by night; he forgot to sleep and journeyed ever northwards. In Oulu he boarded another train, bound for Norwegian Lapland. The sun grew cool as the train gained the Arctic Circle; the vast forests mocked him, the crystalline waters of the fjords witnessed his pain.

And then, the train broke down in a desolate spot. The guards marched into the compartments, informing the passengers that they would have to wait two days for a replacement train. But there was nothing to worry about, they said, food was plentiful and free, the weather was mild.

Preferring the silent evergreens to the company of his fellow passengers, the youth wandered into the nearby forest. Gathering dry spruce twigs and bark from the birch trees, he built a fire and for two days he sat by its flames and read Homer. He read that when Odysseus and his sailors reached Circe's island, they came upon a stone house in the midst of a knotted forest, and were met by wolves and lions made meek by magic. From within the house there wafted the enchanting voice of the goddess of the island. Only Eurylochus, who was a kinsman of Odysseus, escaped Circe's charms and magic spells. As for the other sailors: they were transformed into swine. Alerted to the danger by Eurylochus and aided by Hermes, Odysseus subdued the goddess and forced her to be his lover. He remained on the island for months until his warriors – who had regained their human form – grew nostalgic for home. Circe knew she had to let Odysseus go, but she warned him that he would never gain home by sailing directly to Ithaca. To return home, he and his men would have to journey into the underworld, through the land of Death.

The youth reached the port of Narvik a month after his departure from Stockholm. Standing at the entrance to the northernmost railway station in the world, he knew the futility of further travel. That day, he sat on a lonely bench in the drizzling rain and watched as the boats bobbed up and down in the small harbour. At last, as the faint rays of the hidden sun sang their farewell, he lay himself down on a pebbled beach and wept.

He returned to his native Copenhagen, where he enrolled as a medical student at the university. The weeks flowed into months and the months soared into years. He graduated, became a general practitioner on the Gammeltorv Square and his professional years saddened into decades. He loved one woman and then another, and each time, when his love was exhausted, he cast his mind back to the girl with the flaming red hair. Later, he married, divorced, remarried. His second wife gave birth to three children: two boys, one girl. He achieved all of his earthly ambitions and was recognised by his friends as a good father, a devoted husband and a competent medical man; his life became the model of a perfectly ordinary life, the kind of life that is not worth narrating.

In his sixty-fifth year, he retired and not long after he began to lose his memory. He forgot the past; he could not remember the highlights of his professional career; he forgot the name of his wife and the names of his children. In time, he forgot himself and did not notice when his wife died and his two sons deserted him. Only his daughter stood by him in his very old age and in the end, in his ninetieth year, even she abandoned him, leaving him in the care of nurses in a home for the elderly on the northeast coast of Denmark.

On the day he died, long thin arms of powdery sunlight crept into the long hall where the elderly residents gathered after breakfast, and where the more fortunate would be visited by a friend or a family member. The old man from Copenhagen sat in a wheelchair by a high window that looked onto the windswept beach, a blanket warming his lap. Vague sounds reached his ears: footsteps in the hall, a door opened and then shut, a chair scraped the wooden floors, soft voices fluttered about and – in the distance – the sad low tones of a solitary church bell.

A tall woman of about thirty-five had come into the hall with her daughter – a lively child with earth-brown hair and eyes like black moons. It was the girl's fourth birthday and the mother had brought her to see Grandma, a delicate white-haired woman who always sat alone in a corner. But the child was more interested in studying the expressions of the old folks than in anything that Grandma had to say. Suddenly, her eyes alighted on the old man from Copenhagen, and, led on by an irresistible curiosity she walked up to him with deliberate steps and said, "What's your name?"

My name, he pondered, *what is my name?* But it had been many years since he could remember anything about himself.

"Do you live here?" the child continued.

He puzzled: *Is this my home?* He looked about him, searching the withered faces of the old.

"Who are you?" she insisted. Her voice had risen ever so slightly.

The old man from Copenhagen turned his gaze upon the child. Something in her expression stirred the inner chambers of his being, releasing an image from the lost kingdom of his youth. He leaned forward and extended a wrinkled bony hand; but the girl stepped back and the image was gone.

"Mama! – Mama!" she cried.

The mother came running. Wrapping her arms around her daughter, she said, "I'm here, darling, I'm here. I was just talking to Grandma." Then, turning to the old man, she said in a hostile tone, "I'm sorry if my daughter has troubled you."

He watched while mother and daughter wandered away from him, hand in hand, and sat with Grandma for the rest of the morning. His eyes lingered on the child, searching that young face for a clue to the mystery of his existence, unaware that by evening he would breathe no more. Then, the women said their farewells: mother and daughter were departing. He watched them as they made their exit, realising at last that something was slipping through his grasp, that a fragment of his being was about to be lost. Then, at the last glance, as the girl and her mother pushed open the door to the outside world, a stray thread of sunlight fell on the girl's countenance, turning the brown of her hair into red flames.

In a dark corner of his soul, a rusty gate swung open, and his youth, long since buried in the land of the dead, came back to haunt him: the taxi on the Stockholm pier, Homer's verses in his bag, the immensity of the Baltic sky – and the beautiful stranger with the burning red hair, his silent companion on the night sea journey to Turku.

© George Berguño 2009

Download classic **Dark Tales** e-books...

...at **www.DarkTalesBooks.com**
and **www.DarkTales.co.uk**